THE NECROMANCER'S LIBRARY

ELLIE JORDAN, GHOST TRAPPER, BOOK TWELVE

by

J. L. Bryan

Published March 2020
JLBryanbooks.com

Acknowledgments

Thanks to my wife Christina and my father-in-law John, without whom I would be a full-time parent struggling to write at odd hours.

I appreciate everyone who has helped with this book, including beta readers Robert Duperre and Apryl Baker (who are both talented authors themselves). Thanks to my copy editor, Jason Sizemore of Apex Book Company, and proofreaders Thelia Kelly and Barb Ferrante. Thanks to Claudia from PhatPuppy Art, who created the great cover art for this book, and her daughter Catie, who's done all the lettering on the covers for this series.

Thanks to my agent Sarah Hershman and to everyone at Tantor Media and Audible who have made the audio versions of these books. The audio books are read by Carla Mercer-Meyer, who does an amazing job.

Thanks also to the book bloggers who's supported the series, including Heather from Bewitched Bookworms; Mandy from I Read Indie; Michelle from Much Loved Books; Shirley from Creative Deeds; Katie from Inkk Reviews; Lori from Contagious Reads; Kelly from Reading the Paranormal; Lili from Lili Lost in a Book; Heidi from Rainy Day Ramblings; Kelsey from Kelsey's Cluttered Bookshelf; Abbie from Book Obsession; Ashley from Paranormal Sisters, Ali from My Guilty Obsession, and anyone else I missed!

Most of all, thanks to the readers who have supported this series as it continues to grow.

Chapter One

"Those cows over there are super cute. Look, Ellie!" Stacey said, as we passed one of the countless cow pastures lining the highways of middle Georgia. Her short blonde hair ruffled in the warm breeze of the old van's heating vents. Stacey was over the moon to be out of the city and into a deeply rural area of the state—the farmlands of eastern Georgia, a region relatively unknown to both of us.

It had been over three hours since we'd set out from Savannah to meet with this potential client, who lived quite a bit inland, though not all the way to Atlanta. We'd passed many cows, and many horses, and many donkeys, and Stacey apparently wanted to make sure I didn't miss any of them.

"My grandparents' place is just like this," Stacey said, continuing to talk. "All fields and woods. I've barely seen a building that wasn't a barn or church in the last hour. What town are we going to again?"

"Philomath," I said. "A tiny old town from the 1800s. There was a rich-kid prep school there in the nineteenth century, but it's long gone. Now there's just a few scattered old plantation houses."

Stacey shook her head. "We're going to be really isolated out here, Ellie, so I hope this ghost isn't one of the rough ones. Maybe it's an innocent, squeaky little puppy ghost. One that plays with haunted balls and does cute little puppy-ghost tricks. Yes, he does! Yes, he does!"

"And digs up bones in the back yard?" I asked.

"You had to make it creepy." She frowned and stopped petting her imaginary ghost dog.

"I just hope we aren't driving all the way out here over a loose floorboard or a draft. We can't bill much if there's actual ghost to clear out. And we could use the business." Things had been quiet around the office in recent weeks, though that wasn't the worst thing after some of the monsters we'd faced around Christmas, including my own most personal of demons. January and February had turned slow, and our calls had been more of the squeaky-door than shrieking-ghost variety.

This call had sounded different.

Well, technically, it was an email, but the person contacting us had described problems not easily explained by a dripping faucet or a squirrel in the attic. Or even a squirrel in the faucet.

"Look at those baby goats!" Stacey exclaimed as we whizzed past another farm. "So fuzzy and squeezable."

"Are we there yet?" I glanced at the map app on my phone, mounted on the van's dashboard to keep things hands-free.

We'd passed the last town ten or fifteen minutes earlier, a tiny, cute, old-fashioned brick place called Washington—I assume named after the president, though I didn't look that up or verify it in any way. Could have been Booker T. or Denzel for all I knew. A clock tower had overlooked the little postcard-photo town square like in *Back to the Future*.

Beyond that, things had turned purely rural, becoming the woods and farms were now passing, Which are nice enough if you're, say, out for an autumn walk with a hot guy carrying a thermos of equally hot cider, but not if you're running through the forest in the middle of the night while some invisible thing chases after you. Sometimes nature is more *Evil Dead* than Snow White, in my experience, but then my experience is probably skewed.

"Maybe we'll get to bonfire and camp," Stacey said as we passed a thick, shadowy stand of woods.

"Can you use 'bonfire' as a verb?"

"Oh, yeah. As in 'it's chilly tonight, let's bonfire.' Or 'let's bonfire and tell ghost stories.' You can bonfire and drum circle—"

"I'm gonna stop you there," I said, turning up the music a little—Lana Del Ray, Stacey's pick, but I was enjoying it. Definitely better than a drum circle.

The pine trees became thicker and older, the roads rough and bumpy. The only signs of civilization were occasional mailboxes and dirt driveways that snaked out of sight into the woods.

We turned onto the roughest road of all, pitted and potted so badly it rattled and bounced our old blue van the whole way. Nobody had maintained this road in years. We passed the gray shell of a two-story plantation house with empty sockets for windows and doors, its front steps rotted away, its bottom level half-swallowed by weeds and spindly trees.

"No cute animals here," Stacey murmured as we passed an overgrown field ringed with collapsing fence posts and barbed wire.

Then we arrived.

Maybe it was just the late afternoon light, but the day seemed darker as we approached the house ahead, the brick mailbox marked with our client's address in crooked brass numbers. We turned off onto the broad half-circle gravel driveway, which was more weeds than gravel.

It was a huge Greek Revival house, with four massive box columns across the front and a balcony above the front door. It was old, but not a sun-bleached ruin like the last house we'd passed. Abandoned gardens full of briers filled most of the space between the house and the fields, which had been neglected for so long that tall firs had sprouted up in them.

"Wow," Stacey said, looking over the aged structure. "How old do you think it is? The plantation days?"

"It's definitely antebellum."

"It must cost a fortune to maintain," Stacey said as we parked on the gravel drive, next to a beige

Toyota Tercel that looked almost as ancient as our van.

"Maybe that's why so much of it's sealed up." I opened the door and stepped out into the shadows of the house. It seemed like it had been cared for with something of a triage approach in recent decades, fixing only the worst problems and letting others linger. The white paint was peeling, poison ivy crept up the walls, and most of the windows on the western side were shuttered tight.

Normally it's a pleasant feeling to step out of a car at the end of a long road trip, knowing that whatever might lie ahead, at least it wouldn't involve sitting and staring at the road any longer. That goes double when you've departed the city traffic for fresh green country air.

However, this beautiful but decaying old mansion, its white facade tinted orange and red by the slumping afternoon sunlight, gave me a tight feeling in my gut and a sudden urge to jump right back into the van and hightail it out of there.

"I just got the total creeps," Stacey whispered, her eyes looking over the expansive house. Vines grew along the sides and corners, another sign of neglect. The trees nearby were shaggy with poison ivy.

Wide brick stairs led up to the portico, framed by massive columns holding up a triangular pediment roof. The overall effect was like an ancient temple, erected for some mysterious purpose out in these overgrown fields, its crumbling condition indicating that its priesthood and its god had long fled.

I shook off those thoughts as best I could. The whole point of Greek Revival style is to resemble ancient Greek temples, of course, so the feeling that the house loomed over us like a dark temple wasn't so mysterious. Still, it did look forbidding in that reddish light, the pointed roofline and sprawling wings outlined against the darkening sky like something predatory.

"Don't let your mind play tricks," I said. "Creepy doesn't mean haunted. Facts, not feelings. If we need feelings, we call a psychic."

"Yeah, too bad Jakeroo is slammed with tax season. It's not a good time of year for him to try to get away from work. And, you know, that was a solid three-hour drive here."

"I'm definitely aware," I said, giving my back a stretch before approaching the front door. "What if we really, desperately need Jakeroo?"

She winced, I assume at me repeating the pet name. "He says if we really, desperately need him, he might be able to sneak out here on a Saturday night."

We made our way carefully up the steps, watching for loose bricks. Apparently keeping up the main approach to the house landed in the top level of house-maintenance triage and was deemed worthwhile, unlike peeling back the poison ivy or repainting.

I pressed the front doorbell. The button and plate were simple, functional brass, no attempt to be ornamental or look like some deity's divine doorbell, as though the house's era of austerity had set in by the time electricity arrived.

The woman who answered looked somewhere in her late twenties, like me. Black braids framed her pretty but tense face. Her dark, tired eyes stared at me through bottle-thick glasses. She wore a long coat over a faded vintage dress and patched old jeans, an eclectic ensemble that seemed suitable for a young academic. From her emails, I knew she was a graduate student and teaching assistant at the University of Georgia, about thirty miles from the house.

"Can I help you?" she asked, frowning and completely guarded, as if she'd been expecting no one at all.

"Hi. I'm Ellie Jordan, and this is Stacey Tolbert. We're from Eckhart Investigations in Savannah. May we speak with Cherise Edmunds?"

"That's me," she said, looking more troubled rather than relieved. "What's this about? I sent in that car payment."

Feeling awkward, and more than a little confused, I said: "We had an appointment for six p.m. today."

"What kind of appointment?"

Now I was getting annoyed. "We exchanged several emails with a 'Cherise Edmunds' who asked to meet us at this house at this time. She was very specific about the time, because we wanted to come in the morning instead, as we drove a hundred and ninety miles to get here. And now we're here."

"Emails?"

I reached out to Stacey, who smiled gently as she

brought the emails up on her tablet and showed them to Cherise. "Right here, ma'am. Five messages from someone calling herself Cherise Edmunds. We're supposed to investigate some, well, troubling issues with the property?"

Cherise read over the tablet, her lips pressing tightly together as she rapidly absorbed the text. Finally she looked up at Stacey, then at me.

"Would you excuse me for a moment?" she asked, her tone suddenly angry. Without waiting for a response, she stepped back and heaved the heavy dark slab of the door back into place.

We could hear her yelling at someone inside, though we couldn't make out the words.

Stacey and I looked at each other, at a loss for words of our own.

Chapter Two

"I feel like the intros could have gone better," Stacey said. She glanced uncertainly around the portico and its high columns. The house, even in its heyday, had tried to be impressive more than beautiful, everything about it heavy and bold like a newspaper headline. "Maybe we should head back to the van for water and snacks? Or even back home to Savannah?"

"Maybe so." I turned and looked out over the overgrown front yard to the pitted old road and the fields of brambles and scrub pine beyond. It hadn't been obvious before, but now I could see how the house had once looked out over gardens and fields of crops, a commanding position from the top of an incline almost too subtle to discern.

"If we start driving now, we can get home before midnight," Stacey said. "Which sounds like a great plan to me, honestly. Never mind how freaky this place already makes me feel—and it's going to be so much worse after that sun finishes setting— the facts and evidence plainly show this lady doesn't want us here. Sounds like somebody pranked her. And the sooner we remove ourselves from that awkwardness, the sooner we can be back at our homes, in our slippers, watching our Netflixes."

"You make a strong point." I listened, hearing voices yell distantly inside the house. The massive vault-weight front doors kept it all fairly muffled. "Let's give it five minutes."

"Any chance of whittling that down to two?"

"Three." I shrugged and strolled along the wide portico, seeing what I could see. There was no seating out front, though I suppose a couple of rocking chairs might throw off the austere, regal, home-to-a-minor-deity look the house was meant to convey. Hanging a porch swing from the roof overhang, about three stories up, was probably a daunting proposition, too. Maybe the balcony, supported by the two central columns, would have been a safer bet, but that would have interfered with the approach to the dark, heavy front doors.

Thorny bushes grew up around the porch and over the edge of it—roses, but not in bloom, so they looked more like razor wire. Beyond that lay an old barn half-swallowed by the woods.

It was growing darker and colder fast, and clearly

we weren't wanted here. The apprehensive, knotted feeling in my gut only grew stronger.

"Okay, let's go," I finally told Stacey. "Before they call the police on us or shoot us as trespassers."

"Great idea!" Stacey bolted to the brick steps, as eager to escape as I was.

Then one of the heavy doors creaked open. The woman named Cherise stood there, looking furious. "Did y'all really drive all the way from Savannah?"

"Yes, ma'am," I replied.

"Please don't call me that."

"Okay, sorry. Just trying to be polite."

"I don't think that's necessary after what we put you through. Why don't you come in for a minute? I have some tea and a couple of cookies. It's the least I can offer after Aria's prank."

"Who?" I asked.

"My baby sister." Cherise grunted as she hauled the massive dark door open wider.

A teenage girl, maybe thirteen or fourteen, stood inside, her features dark and pretty like her sister's but currently twisted into an angry scowl, presumably from the heated argument.

"Hi," the girl said, looking carefully at us while we entered.

"Don't just say hi! Apologize," Cherise told her.

The teenage girl rolled her eyes, in standard teenage fashion. "I'm sorry," she said without an ounce of sincerity. "Sorry my sister's a screaming nutcase."

"Don't make it worse," Cherise said.

"How much worse can it get?" Aria snapped

back. "I already live in the world's scariest house in the middle of the woods. I already have to go to school with a bunch of weird country kids who all hate me. I already have you calling me crazy, when you're the one who's crazy, pretending nothing's wrong with this house—"

"Enough." Cherise turned to me. "I am sorry. Why don't y'all have a seat, and I'll be right out with the tea?" She gestured toward an open door to a front parlor. Then she grabbed her sister by the arm. "Come on."

"Sure thing," I said, which sounded awkward, but so was watching family members fight with each other, especially when I was the object of the fight, for reasons unknown.

Because of that whole situation, I didn't even comment on how awestruck I was by the entrance hall. Bookshelves lined the walls from the age-warped hardwood floor to the high ceiling. They even ran up alongside the long, narrow staircase to the second floor. The entire hall was a bit narrow because of the protruding bookshelves on either side, but it was glorious; I was easily looking at a thousand books or more.

I nodded at Stacey and we headed into a front parlor furnished with antique wingback chairs accompanied by end tables with lamps. Books filled every space from floor to ceiling here, too.

"This is amazing," I whispered to Stacey, looking over the antique books on one shelf. The faded letters on the leather bound spines told me they held the *Iliad*, the *Theogeny,* and the plays of Aeschylus, among other ancient Greek works.

"I know." Stacey looked at her phones. "Weak cell service, but there's WiFi. Did she mention the password?"

"It's like the whole house is a library," I said.

"Yeah, you probably love that," Stacey said. "It definitely looks nice. Like a fancy club from another age, when people would sit around reading for fun."

"Lots of people still read for fun."

"Oh, yeah. Lots. There is seriously no signal."

I sighed, resisting the temptation to pull out antique volumes and leaf through the yellowed old pages. This room seemed devoted to the ancient Mediterranean, full of collected writings from Greece, Rome, and Egypt. A faded map on the wall illustrated Mare Nostrum, or Our Sea, as the Romans called the Mediterranean, with every city and province labeled in Latin. It was riddled with small holes and preserved behind glass, clearly an antique, though surely it didn't actually date back to ancient Rome.

"Here we go." Cherise entered the room with a pitcher of iced tea and a plate of small, lumpy cookies, badly charred around the edges. "Some are a little burnt."

"My sister's a total disaster in the kitchen," Aria informed us, following behind with mismatched glasses for us.

"Go to your room, Aria," Cherise said.

"No way. These are the ghost experts. And that creepy place upstairs is not, and never will be, *my* room. It's some dead person's room."

"I told you, it was just one of Dr. Marconi's guest rooms—"

"Not always," Aria said. "It was somebody's bedroom in the past. A lot of somebodies who are probably *all* dead now and haunting the room together—"

"Stop it!" Cherise snapped. She looked at us. "I am sorry, Miss—uh, I didn't quite retain your name —sorry about that, too, I'm bad with names—"

"Ellie Jordan." I sipped the tea, found it shockingly sweet. "This is good."

"Anyway. I know you didn't drive all the way here for tea and cookies, but it was the least we could do before sending you on your way—"

"You are not doing that!" Aria shouted. "They're here now. Why not let them take a look?"

"Because I already said no to this. You're not forcing me into changing my mind."

"You mean the way you forced me to move here, away from all my friends?"

"Aria—"

"There is something in this house!" Aria turned away from her sister and stalked toward me. "Yes, I wrote you pretending to be my sister, but only because I didn't think you'd listen to a kid. But everything I said about this house is true. I didn't lie about that. It's not a *prank*. We need *help*."

"I am so sorry," Cherise said. "This is all part of her acting out because we moved here. I didn't want to move into this old place, either, but our rent and utilities were a huge part of our budget. Now we can pay down debt, maybe even save a little. It's not forever."

"Yeah. Just a year out of my life," Aria said. "My whole senior year."

"You're in eighth grade, Aria."

"My senior year of *middle* school! And I'm stuck at Country-Fried Nowhere Don't Know Anyone Middle."

"I hear they have a great theater program at Country-Fried Nowhere," Stacey said, clearly trying to lighten the mood. "And the marching band's pretty impressive. The football program..." She trailed off as Aria showed no sign of finding this amusing.

"Where did you live before?" I asked.

"Athens," Aria said quickly. "It's a town with, you know, an actual *town*, not just a gas station twenty minutes away. And the university and all that. It's, like, pretty cosmopolitan, for a small town. And before that, we lived in Columbus, but that was before Momma died—"

"They don't need our life story, Aria," Cherise interrupted. "All they need from you is an apology."

"It's fine," I said. "We really do have a lot of experience with the paranormal."

"Toldja they wouldn't call me crazy," Aria said.

"I don't believe in ghosts," Cherise said quickly, as if the conversation were edging into a dangerous area. "I admit this house is isolated, and neither of us like that. And it's large and old, which means a lot of creaking at night—"

"What I saw wasn't just some creaking!" Aria shouted.

"I understand," I said. "To be honest, we often find perfectly rational, natural causes for what people think is a haunting. Our minds tend to personalize impersonal things, to find faces in random patterns, to interpret unexpected noises as voices and footsteps."

"That is completely *not* what's happening," Aria told me. "I'm not crazy. Or stupid."

"I don't believe you are," I said. "Your emails definitely convinced us you were an intelligent and rational adult. My point is, an investigation can set everyone's mind at ease. Collecting evidence, looking at it in the calm light of day, making things objective —these can settle the situation down. Odds are, we won't find anything supernatural, but we will find the root of your problem."

I wasn't totally sure I believed this as I said it; Stacey and I both had bad feelings about this place. We'd both felt such a strong urge to make a fast exit that Cherise's initial rejection of us had come as almost a relief.

Anyway, I hadn't come all this way to run from whatever might be haunting this house. Protecting the living against the evil and restless dead, that's my calling, my only real purpose in life. My intuition, unscientific as it was, told me there was something here, something that might be endangering both of them, and Aria had turned to us out of desperation. I wasn't going to abandon them.

"What kind of investigation?" Cherise asked, looking beyond skeptical.

I told her the usual—thermal and night vision

cameras, motion detectors, high-sensitivity microphones, devices to detect electromagnetic fields and fluctuations.

She did not appear less skeptical. "You put cameras in our house and watch us?"

"Not in bathrooms or bedrooms, obviously, unless those are the trouble spots."

"Mine is," Aria said. "You can stay in my room all night if you want. I don't care. I stay up all night reading anyway, most of the time."

"Which you need to stop doing," Cherise said.

"Maybe once I don't live in a house with a freaky crying ghost."

"There is no ghost!" Cherise replied.

"Then prove it," Aria said. "Let them investigate and prove it. Or do you think they'll prove me right?"

Cherise opened her mouth to continue the argument, then hesitated. "And if I let them stay one night, you'll let this go? Permanently? Is that what it will take?"

"That's right." Aria crossed her arms, glaring. "That's what it'll take."

Cherise looked at me for a long time. "And you're serious about all this, too?"

I nodded.

"All right, I'll do this, only to show my sister there's nothing to fear. But no cameras or anything in or near my room."

"Of course not," I said.

Cherise nodded. "So how do we get this over with?"

"You could tell us a little about the problems you're having. Show us anyplace in the house where you've experienced something abnormal."

"Our life here is abnormal," Cherise said, shaking her head. "And like I said, I don't believe in ghosts. But I agree this house is scary at night. And cold."

"I'll tell you everything," Aria said. "It comes to the hall outside my room."

"You go on," Cherise said. "I'm making dinner. Y'all want some? It's just salad and grilled chicken. And you saw how the cookies turned out."

"No, thank you," I said, hurrying before Stacey could accept. I didn't want to be any more of a financial burden on these people than necessary. "We'll be happy to listen to your sister for a minute."

"Well, she will talk for as long as anybody will listen, if not longer, so y'all enjoy," Cherise said, drawing a scowl from Aria.

"Come on," Aria said. "Let's go upstairs. That's where I hear her at night."

Chapter Three

We headed to the book-lined front hall, which
ended at another set of double doors made from the
same dark, heavy wood as the front doors. I thought
again of ancient temples—the outer courtyard for
the public, the inner sanctum with the pagan idols
sealed off, accessible only to the elite priests.

Aria led us up the long, straight front staircase to
the second floor, lined with more built-in
bookshelves that ran like a timeline of English
literature from *Beowulf* to Shakespeare and up
through Byron and Shelly. Philip Larkin occupied the
final shelf; apparently the late professor wasn't
interested in English poets beyond that.

"You said your sister was hired to organize a

deceased professor's books and papers, but this place looks pretty organized to me," I said.

"These are just the front rooms. The back's a mess."

The upstairs hall was lined with more books. The whole house was a library.

Behind us, the hallway extended to the glass doors of the front balcony. A banister railing walled off the long drop to the stairs we'd just ascended. Experience had taught me to avoid balconies as well as long drops in haunted houses.

Aria pointed at a portrait on the wall featuring a smiling young couple in front of the house's portico, the rose bushes in bloom and trimmed to a much more reasonable size. "That's him. Professor Marconi. My sister started working for him, organizing his books and papers and junk, right before he died."

Stacey snapped a picture while I studied the painting. The recently deceased former owner of this house certainly looked professorial—horn-rimmed glasses, beard, brown woolen jacket. The smiling blonde woman beside him was a ravishing beauty, or at least the painter had portrayed her that way. She wore a puffy silken dress that definitely didn't look like anything from the twenty-first century.

"They seem like a happy couple," Stacey commented. "What happened to her? Is she still around?"

"How would I know? Do you want to hear my thing or not?" Aria asked.

"Of course. Take us through what you've experienced," I said.

Aria led us down the hall, which was dim despite the overhead lights. Ahead, it ended in another pair of heavy dark double doors, which presumably led into the back wings of the house that we'd glimpsed from outside.

Aria didn't lead us all the way to the double doors, but into a spacious bedroom on one side of the hall. It was furnished with a jumbled mixture of antiques, like the rolltop desk at the back, and cheap modern furniture, like the bed with its shiny, badly scratched faux-wood frame. On the bookshelves, any antique books that were supposed to be there had been replaced with a scattering of bright, worn paperbacks featuring teenage girls on the covers, one walking in the woods with a boy, another apparently attending some kind of college for attractive werewolves.

"So, what happens is I'm lying here." Aria sat on the edge of the bed. Heavy curtains draped the windows all the way to the floor, framing the night outside. The floor was bare hardwood. "I'll be reading or doing homework—because I don't sleep much at night since we moved here. I slept like a lamb in Athens, by the way, even though our apartment complex could get pretty sketchy at night.

"Anyway, I hear it late at night, usually way after midnight. She cries. Sobbing, like something terrible just happened to her. The first time, I thought it was the TV in my sister's room. The second time, I thought maybe it *was* my sister crying, so I went to look.

"It was about one or two in the morning, and the house was super dark. And super cold. The heat in this stupid house barely works. My sister's had a guy out to repair it three times and he says nothing's wrong. It's kinda like the thermostat just can't tell when the house is cold. So it's as stupid as everything else here."

I nodded, jotting notes on my pocket notepad. Stacey was recording the girl, too, and snapping pictures of the room, but I always like a little pencil and paper action for myself. "So you heard crying, got out of bed, and the house was dark and cold. What next?"

"I went out in the hall and turned on the lights." Aria stood and headed for the hallway, and we followed her out there. "At first it was quiet, and I almost went back in my room, but I heard it again. This girl crying, bad, like she was scared or hurt. Same as I heard the night before."

She led us to another door, down and across the hall from her own, but didn't open it. "I ran to my sister's room here. Everything out here is guest rooms, three bedrooms and a big weird old bathroom." Aria pointed to the heavy black double doors at the end of the hall. "Reesey says beyond those doors is the master bedroom where the old professor lived, and we're not supposed to go in there. Like I want to go sniffing around some dead old man's bedroom, gross." She kept staring at the doors. "Those doors creep me out anyway. You just know there's something bad behind them."

"Reesey is your sister?" I asked.

"Yeah, I couldn't say 'Cherise' right when I was a kid. So I called her Reesey. Like Reesey's Peesey's candy, which I couldn't say right either."

"Okay. So, back to the crying..."

"I thought it had to be her, since I heard it both nights. I went down the hall. Opened the door to her room. Nope. No movie, no Reesey. She was probably still down in the main library, working late, trying to meet that stupid deadline."

"What deadline?" I asked.

"Just that she has, you know, twelve months to get it all done."

"Or what?" I felt like I was prying too much into their private business, but all of this had apparently been set in accordance with the dead professor's will.

"Or she, I don't know, doesn't get paid everything? I don't really get it." Aria looked uncomfortable. "But if she gets it done sooner, we move out sooner, so I'm glad she's working late."

"So her room was completely quiet?"

"Yeah. I even turned on the lights and looked around. Nothing. I told myself it was just my stupid mind tricking me. So I go back to the hall, and I'm ready to run back to my room... and there it is again. The crying wasn't coming from my sister's room, it never had been."

"Where was it coming from?"

"Further down the hall. So... " She pointed at the dark double doors.

"From the doors?" I asked. "Did you open them?"

"I was thinking about it. I was walking closer, listening for the voice again. I wanted to ask if someone was there, but I couldn't talk, like I was kind of afraid. But I heard the crying again, one more time, and it was obviously on the other side of the door. And then..."

I waited, but she trailed off, staring at the doors. She was trembling.

"Then what?" I asked, gently as I could.

"I saw it. Her, I guess, but it just looked horrible, like a skeleton had come up out of a grave and started walking around. I mean, it was like a dead body. Rotten old rags for clothes. It showed up all at once, just standing in front of those doors as I got there. And its skull eye sockets were *looking* at me."

"Yikes," Stacey whispered.

"That sounds scary," I said, looking at the dark doors and imagining the girl seeing such a thing in the middle of the night. I shivered.

"Uh, yeah," Aria said. "So I ran around the house screaming until I found my sister, down in the main library. She told me it was just a nightmare. I stayed down there with her until the sun came up."

"I'm so sorry," I told her. "Have you heard or seen anything since?"

"*Yes*. The crying comes at night sometimes. Not every night. Sometimes a few nights go by and I think it's all over. I think maybe my sister's right— my imagination, bad dreams, all of it. Then I hear the crying. But I don't go out to check it anymore. I keep my door locked."

"Anything else?"

"*Yes.* One time I saw her, and she wasn't a skeleton. She was almost like in the paintings, a pretty girl with coiled-up braids. Blonde hair, I guess, though she didn't have any color at all when I saw her. She was all white. Not like you, but I mean *white* like zero color, like clouds or flour. She looked so sad.

"I saw her late one night out in the hall. At first I almost thought it was my sister, until I looked right at her. Then I thought it was a regular person, like a living person, who was in our house for some reason. Maybe a friend of Reesey's or something, I don't know. But I kind of knew that was wrong, too, because of the weird color.

"I just froze, I was so scared. I watched her go down the hall toward the doors. And before she got there, she was just gone. It's hard to explain. It wasn't a sudden thing, or a big thing, when she disappeared. It was more like I blinked and missed it. And once she was gone, you know, I was scared but I started wondering if I was just going crazy.

"I ran to Reesey's room, and she *was* there this time, asleep. And she told me it was just a bad dream. I stayed on the chair in her room. She went back to sleep, but not me. I locked her door and sat there staring at it until the sun came up. That was the first day I was almost glad to go to this dumb new school, because at least I got to leave the house."

"Wow," I said. I set down my pencil and flexed my fingers, which had been scribbling furiously. "Did you hear the crying again that night?"

"Not that night, but I still hear it sometimes. I

just keep my door locked when I'm home. What I hate most is when I have to go down the hall to the bathroom." She pointed to the ajar door across from her sister's bedroom.

The bathroom was spacious, about the size of my whole studio loft back in Savannah. People had so much more room for everything out in the country. The antique oval-shaped bathtub had a shower ring and curtain that didn't quite fit right, as if they'd been added decades later. A pair of tall, narrow windows like the ones in Aria's room had become black mirrors with the vanishing sunlight, reflecting ghostly images of me standing in the doorway.

"Have you ever experienced anything in here?" I asked Aria.

"Not *in* here, no. Only on my way here, or on my way back. I hear her crying. One time she's like a lost, helpless girl, the others she's something from *The Walking Dead*."

"Are you sure it's the same entity, not two different ones?"

"How would I know?"

"Okay." I stepped out and closed the door. "Is there anything else you've experienced? Any other part of the house that bothers you?"

"Yeah, literally the whole house bothers me."

"I understand, but—"

"Try going down to the kitchen late at night. I don't, because it feels like somebody's watching you all the way down the hall, all the way down the stairs, the whole way there and back. Like somebody's walking behind you, even when nobody's there. And you'll hit a place that's cold. Cold spots are signs of ghosts, too. Everyone knows that."

I nodded. "Is there any other place you've seen or heard anything unusual?"

"Go back in the southwest library room where my sister does most of her work. There's all kinds of weird stuff back there. Bones. Weird old paintings, old books full of... just sick... " She shivered. "Don't tell my sister I've ever been back there, okay? I'm not allowed."

"Okay." Obviously, we'd have to have a look at the forbidden library room. "We should start by setting up observation gear here in the upper hall. We can use the empty bedroom across from yours as a base to watch and listen. I'd like to have a look in there, too..." I pointed at the dark doors, but Aria shuddered visibly. "But we'll stay out of there for now. Maybe you can show us the rest of the house?"

"Sure. Anywhere but there." Aria looked at the dark doors a final time, then at the big portrait in the hall. "I think it's her, the lady in the picture. Her name's Piper. One of the paintings downstairs is labeled with their names."

"And has she died?"

Aria shrugged. "She's not here anymore, is she?"

"We'll look it up." I studied the portrait of the young couple, wondering how many years ago it had been painted, and what had become of them.

Night was falling outside, and I was eager to set up and get started. With any luck, we could capture some part of what Aria had been seeing and hearing, and determine what might be haunting this sprawling library of a house.

Chapter Four

Typically, I like to fully explore a house and the grounds around it before setting up an observation, and really prefer to do this during daylight hours, but that wasn't happening tonight. Aria, posing as Cherise via email, had begged us to come as soon as possible, and scheduled us to arrive after Cherise returned home from her day job as a teaching assistant in the university history department.

Downstairs, we found Cherise in the kitchen. Even here there were bookshelves, offering recipe books from around the world, plus a few volumes on the medicinal properties of herbs. Cherise sat at the round, rough-hewn kitchen table, picking at a plate of greens and a small piece of unevenly browned chicken.

"How was it?" she asked Aria, in a tone that wasn't particularly welcoming.

"Good. They *listened.*" Aria took a plate and began picking at her own food, not looking any more interested in it than her sister.

"If you're not going home, you may as well sit down." Cherise nodded at me.

"Miss Edmunds—" I began, taking a chair.

"Cherise."

"—we think it would really help your sister if we attempted to document what she's experiencing. We would only focus on the upstairs hall, and maybe a few of the common areas downstairs."

"Nothing in our rooms?" she asked brusquely.

"Definitely not. However... we would also like to see the rest of the house. Get a real understanding of the place. It's a little confusing from the outside."

"It's more confusing on the inside, I can tell you that," Cherise said. "The main library is chaos. I've been at it for two months, and sporadically for about six months before that, and I've barely gotten started."

"Can you explain a little more about your work here?" I asked. "How did you come to work for Dr. Marconi?"

Cherise sighed and put down her fork. She hadn't been eating much, anyway. Neither of them seemed to have an appetite.

"Dr. Philip Marconi was, many decades ago, a somewhat noted professor of history. His particular areas of expertise included folk legends and

mythology. Not exactly religion, but more like...
supernatural alternatives to religion. Magic. His
reputation was based on some early papers exploring
lesser known superstitions and folk tales of the
Deep South, disentangling threads and tracing them
back to their roots, from Western Africa to Ireland
and Scandinavia. His focus included magical charms
and curses."

"Sounds kinda neat," Stacey said.

"From what I understand, he spent his life
collecting all kinds of books, manuscripts, and
artifacts—I don't know where he could possibly
have obtained some of these antique items, and
honestly I wouldn't be surprised if it wasn't entirely
legal. Anyway, he collected and collected, but
somewhere along the way he stopped organizing and
cataloging, and just began piling it all over the place."

"Did his wife pass away?" I asked.

"Yes, that was Piper, the blonde girl from the
paintings. Apparently she died quite a long time ago,
and maybe that led to him teach less and become
reclusive. Don't quote me on that, though, because
Dr. Marconi didn't talk much about his personal life.
He definitely didn't talk about her. I only heard that
from Dr. Anderson, the professor who connected
me with this job."

"How long had Dr. Marconi been retired?"

"I don't know. Many years, maybe decades. I did
not research his personal life, and he certainly did
not volunteer anything."

"What was your impression of Dr. Marconi?"

"I would say he was... grouchy. I thought he

didn't like me very much, but he hired me. I came out occasionally, on weekends, to start the job of organizing the chaos. He didn't seem to be in any particular hurry about it when he was alive, just told me to come when I felt like it. Which is why this deadline is killing me."

"Your sister mentioned a deadline, but she didn't explain it," I said.

"Twelve months, or she gets nothing! It's like a bad reality show." Aria scowled.

"Watch yourself," Cherise warned her. "I don't get nothing. I still get the monthly stipend and free use of the house during those twelve months. But there's a bonus if I get it done in twelve, which would really help us out. The bonus is more than all twelve months of the stipend, so it more than doubles my pay. I'm working night and day trying to get this done, but there's all kinds of books and manuscripts and even scrolls out there, in all kinds of languages, and a lot of them have no paperwork with them.

"So, yeah, I'll just puzzle out some fifteenth-century handwritten Cyrillic so I know how to sort and catalog this crumbling old heap of parchment. Oh, and by the way, when I finally decode it, it'll turn out to be instructions for digging up a dead man's skull and rubbing it with potions to learn his secrets, or something equally pleasant. Because the professor took an interest in some very dark subjects in his old age. I'm sifting through weird funerary rites, spells for raising dead souls from hell and pulling them down from heaven. There's instructions for summoning demons, and for how to get a corpse to speak as long as it's still warm—"

"Stop it!" Aria shouted, standing up. "I don't want to hear this."

Cherise looked startled, too, as if she'd been desperate to unload and forgotten Aria was in the room. "I'm sorry, Aria. I may not be seeing the kinds of things you're seeing, but this place is getting to me, too."

Aria drew headphones from her jacket pocket and went to sit with a tablet by the kitchen's brick fireplace, where a few logs were burning. Most teenagers might have headed up to their rooms at this point to escape the adults, but she obviously had reasons to avoid being upstairs alone after dark.

"Do you think this could be my fault?" Cherise asked me. She'd lowered her voice, but was also clearly counting on the girl not hearing us through her headphones. "I really didn't expect the professor's work to be so disturbing. His book of Southern lore talked a little about ghosts, but also about healing spells and love charms, and mostly about the cultural traditions, like Gullah root doctors, or the Yunwi Tsunsdi, the magical tiny people of Cherokee legends. His early work was about preserving a record of vanishing traditions. I assumed I'd be looking at that kind of thing. When he first brought me in, the materials I cataloged were quite a bit lighter, in fact, with lots of transcripts of traditional stories and oral histories.

"When he died, it was a shock. It was even more of a shock when his attorney contacted me with the terms of his will. It seemed like a windfall at the time—no rent and a second income? I hadn't really looked at the Tomb Room at that point."

"The what?" I asked.

"That's what I call it. All those manuscripts about death

gods, the underworld, raising the dead. And there's bones in there, with inscriptions and paintings. Animal bones, maybe. I hope. There could be anything hidden in those heaps." She shook her head. "I can't believe I agreed to this. But we can't afford to stop. We need the extra paycheck."

"I understand. You're in a tough spot."

"Even if..." Cherise went quiet and shook her head, as though in disbelief. "If it's what *you* think it is—"

"I haven't personally observed anything yet," I said.

"—what Aria thinks it is, anyway. Even if it were real, is it always necessarily bad? Isn't every old place said to be haunted?"

"Hauntings are common, but most are benign," I said. "You could live in a haunted house for years and only encounter the ghost once or twice, if it's not active or low energy. They tend to dwell in the dark places of the home that people usually avoid. But sometimes the entities are dangerous."

"It's hard not to work in the big library every night without thinking about how he died in there," she said, her voice soft.

"Who died in there? The professor?"

"Yes. He fell from the third-story walkway in the library. The banister broke. It was a long fall, and he was elderly." She glanced at the hardwood floor, which wouldn't have offered a soft landing.

Stacey and I looked at each other in alarm. Household accidents involving a small push and a lot of gravity are a common way for ghosts to act out murderous intent. If the house had an active haunting, a recent accidental death could be a major red flag.

"I didn't realize he'd died in the house," I said. I was torn between trying to explain what I knew and not trying to come across as someone trying to frighten her. Cherise hadn't invited us here, and the idea of avoiding the whole situation by deciding to call us paranoid superstitious kooks and kicking us out had to be tempting for her.

I was scared of triggering that response, which would leave the two of them alone with any dangerous spirits that might be in the house. Not that I'd concluded any were here, but as the Magic 8-ball sometimes tells us, signs were starting to point to Yes.

"We'll need to look at the main library," I said. "And this 'tomb room.'"

"That's actually the western wing of the main library."

"The side of the house that's shuttered up?" I asked.

"Yes. It gets very dark in there. There's a chandelier, but it doesn't work."

"We also need to investigate the rest of the upstairs. Beyond the dark doors."

Cherise didn't reply to that. She tapped her sister on the shoulder to come with us, but Aria opted to stay near the small kitchen fire. Smart move. The kitchen often has the strongest, freshest, most positive life energy in the house. Ghosts usually prefer the dark and less traveled spots, haunting attics and basements among the not quite discarded artifacts of the past.

While the sisters spoke briefly, I quietly tugged open a sliding door and had a peek into the dining room. A long black table for twelve sat under a silver chandelier that could have held a major fire hazard's worth of candles. A cold, empty stone fireplace backed up to the kitchen one. Overall, the theme continued of heavy materials with minimal adornment.

Another portrait of the young Marconi couple hung over the fireplace, much bigger than the one in the upstairs hallway. This one showed them in autumn, surrounded by richly colored trees, the house in the background.

"They sure liked getting their portraits painted," Stacey whispered, snapping a few pictures.

Cherise took out a large key ring and led us, with clear reluctance, out of the kitchen and down the first-floor hallway. More poetry and literature lined this hall, a fair amount of it French or Italian, followed by a section of biographies.

She paused at the pair of dark doors at the back of the hall, as though reluctant to go on. "I ask that you not touch anything in the library rooms. Some of it is quite old and fragile, and you'd be surprised how precariously the professor left all of it stored. Try to keep to the established paths, and watch your step, too, because there's plenty of tripping hazards. It gets worse the deeper you go."

"Thanks for the warning," I said.

She nodded and heaved open the door.

I'd thought the book-lined front hall was impressive, but what lay beyond those dark doors stirred as much envy as it did fear of whatever dangerous entities might dwell in the home.

"This is the reading room," Cherise said, indicating a room with numerous lamps, small tables, and matching leather sofa and chairs. The shelves here offered a small selection of books and a number of periodicals arranged by year and date, mostly academic publications. "The fireplace over here was bricked up. Maybe he wanted to protect the collection from any risk of smoke damage."

"A room just for reading," I said. "I guess the lawn chair on my balcony is my reading room."

She smiled thinly and led us past a small study, with an impressive desk and various fancy-study must-haves like an antique telescope and globe.

The hallway ended at an immense three-story room, honeycombed with bookshelves from the floor to the dark, distant recesses of the high ceiling. A maze of narrow walkways and staircases nearly as steep as ladders connected the floor to the upper reaches of the bookshelves.

Squinting, I discerned the glint of chandeliers in the cavernous darkness high above, but Cherise left these turned off. Probably hogged a fortune in electricity, if they worked at all. Instead, she touched a wall switch that illuminated several lamps scattered through the room.

"He called this his hanging garden of books," Cherise said. "Unfortunately, a good deal of it is more like a jungle."

I saw what she meant. Ahead of us lay heaps of unsorted materials piled on tables, on chairs, on the floor, crammed haphazardly into half-empty bookshelves. It was nearly a solid wall of old books, yellow papers bound with twine, loose yellow papers bound with nothing, not to mention shipping crates and wooden boxes of all sizes. A black jackal-headed statue with gilded ears and obsidian eyes stared out solemnly from among the stacks nearby, a statue of Egyptian death god Anubis drowning in paper and packages like an overwhelmed postal worker at Christmas.

The situation grew worse as I looked west, toward the shuttered-up side of the house. Precarious-looking stacks were piled much too high.

"Don't touch anything," she reminded us before leading us down a narrow, twisting path through heaps of unsorted papers.

"It's *Hoarders* meets *Book TV*," Stacey whispered, taking pictures.

"Is this where Dr. Marconi died?" I asked.

"He fell from the top walkway." Cherise stopped to point upward.

I gazed into the dimness above, my eyes slowly adjusting to it. There were two levels of narrow walkways running alongside the upper-story bookshelves, connected by a jumble of staircases, like a game of Chutes and Ladders designed by M.C. Escher.

"You can see the broken railing where he fell," Cherise said. "They tied it off with rope. The attorney said someone would be out to fix it eventually. It's been two months now. I wouldn't go up there at all if I were you. Those old walkways are half the reason I don't allow Aria in here. Climbing around on those would be tempting for a bored kid, but any of it could come crashing down."

With my gaze, I traced what must have been the

path of the man's fall from the broken railing down to a floor rug half-buried in collapsed stacks of paper and clutter. "He must have landed there," I murmured.

Cherise shook her head. "Poor old man, living alone out here with nobody. I heard his housekeeper found him, and he'd been lying there two or three days."

I shivered. I may have envied the late professor's library, but I didn't envy Cherise having to work in the place where he'd died. Though I guess it had become my workplace for now, too.

"The really disturbing material is through here. Don't touch anything," she reminded us before leading us down a final narrow, twisting path through heaps of unsorted papers to a solid wall of bookshelves.

Cherise reached into a bookshelf and touched an odd little keyhole built into the back, where a book could have easily concealed it, though none did at the moment. She slid a key into place and turned it.

With some effort, she rolled aside an entire section of bookshelves, which turned out to be a concealed door into a dark hidden chamber beyond. I don't suppose any extravagant home library would truly be complete without a secret door built into it somewhere.

"This is where I was told to begin," she said. "They said my catalog would be evaluated after twelve months."

"By whom?" I asked.

"They didn't say."

The hidden chamber was cold, even more so
than the rest of the house. It was three stories as
well, with more of the walkways and ladders, but
divided by a solid wall from the rest of the library.

More densely packed and completely unsorted
papers and books waited here, along with an
assortment of strange artifacts. Dusty glass cases
held the bits of bone Aria had mentioned, some
adorned with faded red paint and crumbling
feathers, others carved into strange shapes. One jar
held the coiled skeleton of some horned lizard.
Another held a few brown recluse spiders, corked
inside, surely dead long ago from suffocation or
starvation. Strange statues were scattered among the
collection, too; some looked Aztec, others Middle
Eastern, and still others I couldn't begin to guess.

An enormous squarish old volume of leather
and parchment lay open on the least cluttered table,
next to an open laptop in sleep mode. I clicked on
the desk lamp nearby, then took a sharp breath.

"Whoa, Yikers' Island. And I thought Bosch was
weird," Stacey said.

The open page depicted a gruesome scene, done
in woodcut, of strange people with heads like
horned beasts and reptiles. They danced around a
gravestone and an open pit where a skeleton reached
up as if preparing to climb out of its grave. The
handwritten text around the illustration looked Latin,
blurry and faded with time, interspersed with
equations full of arcane symbols.

"That's not even the worst thing I've seen this
week," Cherise said. "I understand why my sister is

scared, why she's having bad dreams and seeing things. She has come in here at least once—without my permission, obviously—and looked around. What kid wouldn't be scared after seeing all this? As if the strange old house wasn't bad enough. Also, it gets so quiet out here at night. You sometimes hear owls, but not much else. Darkness and silence. Those are prime conditions for your mind to run wild."

"Did she have any problems with nightmares or night terrors before moving here?" I asked. "Any similar experiences?"

"Nothing. I'm sure it's all because of this place." Cherise frowned at the kneeling sacrifice victim in the book.

Another partially-cleared table was covered with black lacquer, dotted with clumps of red and black candle wax. So many candles had burned here that rows of wax stalactites hung from the edges of the table.

"I'm not sure what all this is," Cherise said, joining me by the stacks of wax. "I'm not sure I want to know, honestly."

I looked over the table, then knelt to inspect it more closely. I finally located a keyhole—no knob or drawer pull, just a small keyhole right under the lip of the table, tucked out of sight. "Have you opened this yet?" I asked.

"I didn't know it opened," Cherise said. "There's so much material sitting out, I can't say I've spent much time searching for more."

We tried the keys on her ring until we found the

one that fit.

I folded open the front panel of the desk, revealing a cavity under the tabletop.

Moving carefully, I extracted the items within: a long ivory dagger with odd symbols etched into the gold-plated hilt, a small gold chalice not much bigger than a shot glass on a stem, and a black glass ball framed in a square of wood.

"What is all that?" Cherise asked.

"Ritual objects," I said. "This is not a good sign. It looks like Dr. Marconi wasn't just collecting texts, he was putting them into practice, trying them out."

"But none of it's real, right? I mean, he was crazy to think any of these old superstitions would actually accomplish anything. Right?"

I hedged my answer. "Probably a lot of it's nonsense invented by charlatans and madmen over the centuries. But sometimes, when you reach out in search of spirits, you catch something. It's like fishing – you bait the hook a certain way, you cast the line in a certain place, but you can't always control what comes biting."

"What would these be used for?" Cherise asked.

"The black sphere is probably a scrying mirror."

"Like a crystal ball?" Cherise sounded skeptical as ever.

"Right. Maybe he was trying to see the future. Maybe he was trying to summon entities."

"Entities?"

"Ghosts, demons, angels, pagan gods. You tell me. What do his books cover?"

"Oh, they run the gamut," Cherise said. "I

couldn't say for sure what he was looking for. It seems like he wanted anything dark and twisted."

I felt around inside the ritual table's cavity and brought out a small wooden rod, a little longer and thicker than a pencil, adorned with strange skulls and animal shapes. Behind this I found a leatherbound book.

"What's that?" Cherise said.

I flipped through the book. It was filled with tight, spidery handwriting almost too compact to read. "I'll read it and let you know. My first guess is this is some kind of journal, or maybe a grimoire. Hopefully it will tell us what kind of supernatural activities he was delving into."

"A spell book?" Cherise asked.

"And a pretty gnarly-looking wand," I added, pointing to the carved stick on the table.

"Let me know if you find a house elf, because I could use the help."

"Do you mind if we set up a camera or two in here?" I asked. "Just in case."

"In case what? The dead professor is still hanging around?"

"Well... the kind of activities he was engaged in can increase the odds of paranormal activity—"

"Forget I asked. Just do whatever you think will calm Aria down."

I nodded. "What about the upstairs hall? The section beyond the doors?"

She stiffened. "That's the master suite area. It's close to my room, for one thing. Also, we are meant to leave that area alone, according to my instructions.

I don't want to risk forfeiting this situation. We need the income."

"All right. We'll hold off. My partner and I have plenty to do already, and we want to be settled in and quiet before the early morning hours."

"That would be nice." She sighed. "I'll be honest with you: I don't believe in the supernatural. I don't think you'll find any ghosts in this house, but I'm starting to worry that maybe you will. And then I'll have to rethink everything. Now let's get out of here. I don't like being in this room at night."

We left the tomb room, and Cherise made sure the bookshelf-lined roll-aside door was locked tight behind us.

Chapter Five

It took a few hours to bring in and set up our gear. The spare bedroom upstairs did turn out to be a decent location for our little nerve center of monitors and speakers. Its bookshelves contained impressively old copies of *The Hobbit* and *The Lion, the Witch, and the Wardrobe* as well as *Spells of Magicia* by M. G. G. Jensen.

"Look at that!" Stacey noticed the Jensen book and pulled it from the shelf. "Thurmond Pennefort would freak out if he saw this." We'd once had a client obsessed with the classic fantasy series and its numerous film adaptations, neglecting his family's crumbling one-skyscraper empire while he obsessively created and painted clay figurines and castles to sell at fan conventions.

"It's probably expensive. Put it back."

"Just checking the date. Ooh, 1924, not as old as Thurmond's. Check out the bodice on this wizard princess. You think I could pull off a bodice? It doesn't look like the best outfit for fighting dragons."

"Put it back," I said again. "We still have a lot to do."

We set up assorted gear in the upstairs hall where Aria had most of her experiences—thermal and night vision, microphone and EMF meter, every kind of sensor we had. We also set up a few things in the common areas downstairs and in the library.

Cherise didn't want us to enter the forbidden master suite upstairs, and I didn't push it for fear she'd kick us out. She had made it clear that she viewed us as being there to placate Aria's fears and not much more.

I hoped she was right, but Aria didn't strike me as lying or delusional. Maybe I was wrong about that, because I couldn't read minds. Regardless, the professor's death in the library ratcheted up the potential danger factor.

"All systems okey-dokey," Stacey finally announced. She sat cross-legged in an armchair that she'd dragged from the tightly shuttered window to the open wardrobe, where her array of small monitors occupied the otherwise bare shelves. "It's 11:57 p.m., gear is up, lights are out, clients have gone to bed. It's officially snack time."

"The most important phase of any investigation," I said, trying to keep the mood light even though my stomach was knotted. I had a particularly bad feeling about this case. I told myself to stick with the process and focus on the evidence we collected, if any. It would hardly be professional to start jumping at shadows.

Stacey had brought some really dry granola bars and cans of kiwi-dragonfruit energy drinks. I passed her one of each and reminded myself not to leave her in charge of snacks next time.

Once snack time had passed, we turned off the lights in the room and went into quiet observation time, whispering when we absolutely had to communicate.

"Did I pack any more Stoneground granola bars?" Stacey whispered, apparently deeming this question critical enough to break the silence. I handed her my extra one, since I had no interest in shredding the inside of my mouth with it.

After that, there was much sitting and waiting, watching and listening for any sign of unusual activity. I texted my boyfriend Michael back in Savannah to let him know we'd arrived safely and didn't know when we'd be heading home.

"Why don't they just pop out when we get here?" Stacey complained after an hour or so. "I hate waiting for the ghosts to show up. Especially when it takes days."

"It's part of the job. Like cops on a stakeout, waiting for the perp to do something interesting."

"Yeah, but on cop shows, stakeouts are when the characters reveal their inner selves and bond on a deeper level. You should be saying things like 'I'm getting too old for this job' or 'This city is a sewer of corruption and it's never gonna change' or 'Here's some advice for ya, rookie: never drink liquor before nine a.m., and never order the steak down at Greasy's Diner.'"

"And you should be saying things like 'I became a cop because I believe in the system and I want to help people.'"

"And then you say something like 'Listen to me, kid, you need gristle in your gut and spit in your shoes to do this job.'"

"Let's go back to not talking," I suggested. "We don't want to miss anything."

"Yes. I'll just stare at this hallway while you play games on your phone."

"I'm researching Dr. Marconi."

"Anything coming up?"

"His obituary." I quietly read over the lengthy text.

"Well?" Stacey asked after a minute.

"It mentions he was preceded in death by his wife, Pipette Overbrook Marconi. Pipette? Anyway, it mostly focuses on his work. 'A historian interested in the fading folkways of the past, Marconi collected tales of myth and magic. His 1973 book *Southern Charms and Curses* collected many of these.' Then his teaching career, including visiting professorships at Boston College and the University of London at one point, but he was mostly based at the University of Georgia."

"No hints about, I don't know, why a ghost might push him to his death in his library?" Stacey asked.

"Oh, yep, here in paragraph four. Seriously, let's not jump to conclusions about how Dr. Marconi died."

"But we're both thinking it. How ghosts like to push people, or push things *onto* people—"

"So let's keep an eye out and stay away from steep drops."

"Are you saying..." Stacey dropped into her gruff detective voice again. "'Life's full of steep drops and nasty surprises, rookie. If you don't watch where you're going, you're gonna fall. It's all a metaphor, rookie, a rough, tough metaphor for life in the big rotten city.'"

"You know, I originally had my doubts about hiring someone who went to art school, and I'm glad you're laying those to rest."

"Because of my fantastic tech skills. The guys at SCAD always assumed I would be some clueless blonde, but I could run cables around most of them. I was president of my AV media club in high school. Also president of the hiking club and Tallapoosa Riverkeeper, but I started those. My grandparents really liked for me to be president of things, and it was usually easier to just start something new than take over something old."

I nodded and put a finger to my lips. She did an exaggerated nod and put a finger to her own lips and gave me a thumbs up just to really hammer home that she'd gotten the message. Our presence could change the dynamic of the house enough to send any entities into hiding; staying still and quiet was the best way to minimize that. But it got pretty old.

Searching online, I dug up what I could on the late Dr. Philip Marconi. Memorial pages posted by the university and a few academic and historical societies to which he'd belonged went into greater detail than the obits. Marconi had been eighty-one when he died. His wife Piper had died more than three decades before him.

The internet provided plenty of details about his early and external life, but little insight into his later life, few clues about the man who'd become a reclusive collector of occult manuscripts and memorabilia. The death of his wife was an obvious possible trigger for an interest in the dead; maybe he'd hoped to contact her spirit in the afterlife. Then again, maybe he had already been into it before she died.

A couple of blogs and Instagram accounts had documented the historical buildings of Philomath, particularly The Globe, one of several Greek Revival plantation houses built during the antebellum cotton era.

One place mentioned the current house as The Taylor House and called it less historically significant than The Globe or the preserved church. The house had been "purchased some years after the Civil War by New York native Lucio Marconi, who was then investing in war-cheapened land in Augusta and Athens, and sought to establish himself midway between the cities. His family's extensive changes to the original house have greatly reduced its historical value." The article also noted that "the house is private property. Tourists and photographers are not welcome."

Stacey elbowed me, yoinking me out of my internet rabbit hole. She pointed at the monitor displaying the thermal camera feed from the hallway outside.

"Cold front moving in," Stacey whispered.

A cold spot had formed near the dark double doors at the back of the hall, an area of deep blue no larger than my hand, but definitely there, like a tiny polar vortex floating at doorknob level.

We held our breath, watching.

It didn't move fast, but dead things need not hurry, I suppose. Especially when they're caught in a repetitive loop of activity, as they often are.

The cold spot moved up the hallway, away from the doors.

Nothing appeared on the night vision camera; all seemed perfectly quiet. The sensors in the hallway picked up a falling temperature, but no motion. An EMF meter reflected a minor electrical fluctuation. The temperature and electrical changes together would have been enough to trigger one of our ghost traps to shut, if we'd set one up.

The cold spot drifted up the center of the hallway, growing colder and larger, as if focusing its energy and preparing to act.

It passed Cherise's closed bedroom door and the bathroom across from it.

As it drew even with our door and Aria's, it came to a halt. It lingered in the middle of the hall for a long time, and I wondered if it was sensing our presence.

"Eyeball check?" Stacey mouthed to me after a few minutes, pointing at her own eye. Sometimes the living eye can detect things gadgets can't.

I held up a finger. *Wait.* We were lucky to see anything at all on our first night. I didn't want to run the ghost off by charging out there, unless it threatened our clients.

After a few more minutes, the cold spot began to move again.

It headed toward Aria's door.

I was on my feet, moving toward the door from our room to the hall, my eyes glued to the screen. My hand went to the tactical flashlight holstered in my utility belt, the ghost hunter's sidearm.

The cold spot stopped outside Aria's door. I was ready to charge out there if it passed through into her room.

It didn't, though. It remained stationary, doing nothing at all for several more minutes.

I decided eyeballing it might not be such a bad idea. I motioned to Stacey that I was stepping out.

The hall was definitely colder. Little bumps rose all over my arms, and I felt some apprehension.

I closed the door tightly behind me and stood in near absolute darkness in the hall; anything could have grabbed me and I wouldn't have seen it coming. I kept my flashlight off, though; I was trying to observe the entity, not annoy it into hiding.

My eyes adjusted gradually to the moonlight slipping in through the balcony doors. Watching Aria's bedroom door, I tapped my headset's microphone, signaling Stacey for an update.

"Cold spot's still there," her voice whispered in my ear. "It's looking agitated now, kind of spinning and drifting back and forth.

I stared at the dark rectangle of Aria's closed door, seeing nothing, but definitely feeling the cold.

"Getting colder..." Stacey whispered.

It emerged from the darkness all at once, like a pale fish swimming up from black depths. The eyes and mouth were dark holes, just suggestions of shapes, and the skin was like dry bleached paper stretched taut over bone.

I've seen my share of apparitions, ranging from sad and helpless ghosts to those distorted by their own twisted psychology into monstrous and inhuman things. I can't say I've ever fully grown accustomed to it. The instinctive physical response doesn't help; our bodies can sense something supernatural and dangerous, just as animals can, and tell us to flee.

This particular one was chilling, a partly formed dead thing, and had appeared only inches away, its phantasmal face moving toward me at high speed.

I clicked on my flashlight, more of a defensive reflex than a conscious choice.

Three thousand lumens of full-spectrum white light hit the apparition like a tidal wave, washing through its filmy, frosty substance while it rushed toward me.

For an instant, I had a clearer look at it, and more details did nothing to improve its appearance. It wore a rotten cloth hat, leather tunic and high boots, the clothes cracked and decayed. Much of the entity's shape was hidden under a dark cape or cloak.

Those were the clothes. The entity inside was downright cadaverous, only bits of skin left on its skeletal face with its empty eye sockets, and on its skeletal hands.

Its awful hands reached toward my face—

Stacey burst out and added her light to mine, and the apparition vanished.

"Are you okay? I saw you light up." She swung her searing white light from me to Aria's still-closed door. "Did you see anything?"

"Definitely. Did you?"

"Just that cold spot on the monitor. It rushed toward you!"

"Yeah, I noticed." I clicked off and holstered my flashlight. "I shouldn't have been so jumpy. I spoiled the observation."

"Don't be so hard on yourself. You're lucky it didn't give you a push." Stacey pointed her light at the long, steep front staircase only a few feet away, the long balustrade overlooking it from the upstairs hall where we stood.

"This house has far too many places to get pushed to your death. Nobody's going to be safe here without some serious remodeling." I shook my head. "Let's head back. Maybe we'll get a return visit, but it'll probably lay low after we torched it with all that light."

When we returned to the room, I wrote down as much as I could remember of what I'd seen, and even tried to sketch the unusual bits of clothing it had worn. Maybe this really was a job for an art school graduate.

"I don't know what it was," I told Stacey, "but I don't think it was some lady who died in the twentieth century. It's something older."

Stacey shivered. Older entities tended to be more twisted, more removed from their lives. A centuries-old one might be barely human at all anymore, though it might have grown adept at feeding on the energies of the living.

I would have to convince our reluctant client to allow us to stay and continue the investigation, because there was no way I was going to leave them to face an entity like this on their own.

Chapter Six

We met Cherise and Aria in the kitchen before they could head off to school—Cherise to the university where she both studied and taught, and Aria to her dearly beloathed new middle school. They both had coffee, though Aria was just fourteen, which seemed a little young to me, but then she hadn't been sleeping at night and still had to leave for school before dawn.

Stacey and I had decaf, since it was approaching bedtime for us. The job tends to be a nocturnal one. Ghosts usually avoid sunlight and other intense sources of whole light that can scramble or distort their own weird electromagnetic fields. This isn't an absolute rule, and there's a bit of selection bias because people tend to be home at night and away during the day.

"We observed a cold spot in the hall," I said, catching them up while Stacey replayed the thermal video. "When I went to investigate, it formed a partial apparition and moved toward me in a way that seemed hostile." On the video, the cold spot swelled and deepened before rushing toward my yellow-orange form.

"That's right outside my room," Aria said. "I told you, Reesey!"

"Couldn't that just be a draft?" Cherise suggested. "We have all these furnace problems."

"The temperature fluctuations, possibly, but not the apparition I saw. I believe it fit the description of the cadaverous skeletal one Aria told us about yesterday."

"So you see what I mean!" Aria said.

It was hard to read Cherise's expression behind her glasses. Her lips were pressed tightly together; she obviously didn't like what she was hearing and seeing, but who would?

"My initial hypothesis is that this entity is not the ghost of Piper Marconi, but of someone who lived much earlier." I brought out my description and my clunky sketches where I'd attempted to record what I'd seen—not so much the rotten corpse bits, because ew, but the hints of clothing that indicated we were dealing with a real oldster. "He was wearing a strange hat, and I think maybe a jerkin."

"A what?" Aria asked, snickering a little. At least she was smiling.

"A stiff leather jerkin," I elaborated, mainly so she would snicker more. "A kind of short tunic. Which would be normal if this was the Middle Ages. The other clothes don't exactly look like they came from L. L. Bean, either."

"Is he wearing a dead cat on his shoulder?" Aria asked, pointing at my very poor drawing.

"That's supposed to be a cape," I said.

"Oh. *Oooh.* Sure, I see it. That would have been my next guess, promise."

A thudding sound echoed outside, as if something massive was crashing its way down the street, banging through the potholes.

"The bus." Cherise glanced at the clock on the stove. "You'd better go catch it."

"Can't I stay home today?" Aria asked. "I'm so tired, and the ghost detectives are here. I might actually be able to sleep for once."

"You are not missing school," Cherise said. "All you have to do is walk out there. Hey, at least the bus stops right in front of our house, right? No more hiking six blocks every morning like in Athens."

Aria groaned and pulled on her massive backpack. "It's because no other kids live on this whole stupid road. Did you know that, just because of me, every kid who rides my bus has to get up ten minutes earlier now? Because *they* know it. And they make sure I know it. Every day."

"I'm sorry," Cherise said. "I know your new school is an adjustment."

"I'm not going to adjust. I'm going to stay myself and just wait it out." She walked out toward the heavy front doors.

"She is having the worst time of it," Cherise said, shaking her head once her sister was gone.

"We found something else, but I didn't want to upset her with it. After our encounter with the entity, we went back over the feeds from our gear in the hallway, looking for any corroboration with the cold spot. And... our microphone picked up something. It was too low for us to hear, but Stacey amplified it." I nodded at Stacey.

She pulled up the isolated audio clip and played it.

The voice sounded angry and harsh. I still didn't understand the words.

"I think it's another language," I said. "We'll need help identifying and translating—"

"It's German," Cherise said, quietly.

"Do you... happen to know German?" I asked.

"I'm better with French, Italian, and Spanish," Cherise said. "They're like three pretty sisters. Triplets. German's not my strong suit, but this is clear enough."

"What's he saying?" Stacey played it again, letting it loop every few seconds.

Cherise hesitated. "'Leave this house. You do not belong.'"

The three of us listened to the angry Germanic voice on the recording again, hearing it for what it was: a warning, maybe a threat.

"Okay," I said, and Stacey killed the playback. "Here's what I recommend: we need to investigate further. We need to understand the history of the place, and we especially need to know what Dr. Marconi was up to in that library. I don't think our medieval German guy is someone who lived here, but he certainly feels territorial about the place now. Maybe he was accidentally conjured by Dr. Marconi's occult experiments, or he could be attached to an artifact in the collection."

"There are a couple hundred artifacts in the collection, most with no label or description, in addition to all the books," Cherise said. "Could he be attached to a book?"

"It's possible. Can you help us identify anything from medieval Europe? Artifacts and books."

"I'll do what I can. Now it's about time for me to get to work, so..."

"Sounds good." I rose to my feet, taking the hint. "We'll find a hotel nearby and get some rest."

"You'll probably want to drive to Washington or Athens for that."

"Athens!" Stacey said quickly, and Cherise smiled a little. "I love that place. I went there for an art show in college. And a couple concerts. And various after parties."

"Assuming you're right, and this house is haunted," Cherise said. "Are all ghosts necessarily malevolent?"

"Most aren't. They're just echoes. The malevolent ones aren't as common, but they can be very dangerous."

Cherise nodded; she seemed to be taking it in, thinking about it. Maybe she was adjusting to the idea of the supernatural—the idea that it was real, and the idea that it was happening around her.

We agreed to meet back at the house in the late afternoon, and Stacey and I headed outside to our van. I was feeling tired, but also worried for our clients. The kind of research and rituals that Dr. Marconi had been pursuing could open a paranormal Pandora's box. Maybe they'd even led to his death, and whichever entity had killed him still stalked the hallways of the old house.

Chapter Seven

As it turned out, Athens was our best choice for cheap lodging. The combination of food, gas, and lodging was probably going to be more than what I could realistically charge Cherise for the case, given her existing financial struggles and how reluctant she'd been to have us there at all.

I couldn't leave them alone with something evil and dangerous, though. Cherise and Aria were planning to stay for another ten months.

Stacey and I checked into an extreme budget motel on the highway outside Athens, the kind of place that inspired us to bring our own sleeping bags rather than come in contact with the blankets provided.

I sat on my bed—and sleeping bag—with the lamp on and the old book we'd found hidden in the weird altar-table in the library.

"Some light reading?" Stacey asked. She'd already switched to pajamas and now slid into her sleeping bag on the other bed, her camping pillow under her head.

"I can read this now or I can read this over in the giant spooky old house," I said.

"Good point." She yawned. "But I thought you liked the house. You're usually a megadork for libraries."

"I'd probably feel more megadorky about this one if it wasn't so focused on death and demons," I said. "The front rooms of the house are nice. Almost lulls you into believing it's all going to be Jane Austen and Tennessee Williams."

"Then, pow! *Satan's Book of Forbidden Recipes,*" Stacey said.

I sighed and reluctantly opened the leatherbound book. "Time to peer into the dark side."

"Have fun. Just let me know the Cliff's Notes version, 'kay?" She pulled some kind of organic hemp sleeping mask over her eyes and turned away from the light.

"'Kay," I replied.

Reading through my magnifying glass, I took in the first page.

Invocation

I call upon the wisdom of ancient seers, mystics, prophets,

the wise men and women of the ages,
    the spirits who wander
    the choirs of angels and the hordes of demons
    the old gods and new

"He's really not leaving anyone out," I muttered to myself.

The journal entries were rarely dated, but they began in 1989, not long after his wife's death from a congenital heart defect, about the time he began withdrawing from public life.

His intent was made clear early on:

If only I could speak with my beloved once more—she was taken too soon, too young, and my heart turns to cold ash at the loss of her, where once a great hearth fire of passion blazed—she was my one true path, the angel of my life, lighting the path of the future, a path that now lies as dark and hopeless as the night falling over her grave.

Okay, so it was hard not to feel a little sympathetic. How many times had I wished I could speak with my parents once again, after they'd died when I was fifteen? I'd seen ghost after ghost, but not my parents—not until recently, when portions of them that had been captured by the ghost of Anton Clay were finally freed. Even then, I'd had only glimpse, a flickering moment, as they moved on to the next world along with Clay's other victims, his other captive souls.

Clay was finally gone, and my parents with him. They had all shaped my world in different ways. The loss of my parents had been severe. It remained severe, and I supposed always would.

So I understood why Dr. Marconi might have been tempted to reach out to his deceased wife, feeling her absence acutely every day, every moment.

I skimmed through the pages, trying to form a general sense of the journal before I dove into the details.

His handwriting became increasingly shaky and scratchy over the years, harder to read. He'd copied into the book a variety of incantations and conjuring spells, some in English, some not. Everything was aimed at summoning spirits, contacting the dead, communicating across the barrier between this life and the other side.

An entry that appeared years later, past the point where his writing had turned sloppy and his entries undated, was noticeable because it began with extra large letters: SUCCESS! PRAISE TO ALL HOSTS!

I stopped to read that part, naturally:

...after so many years and failed attempts, I have successfully evoked my beloved. I saw her first in the scrying sphere, then later in the upstairs hall, walking as if to our room. She reached our bed and wept. She is insubstantial, and sometimes alarmingly invisible and silent, but she has returned to me...

Things apparently didn't go as well as he'd hoped, though, because another entry followed, several days later:

My beloved girl continues to weep. She speaks with me some, in fragments, but she cannot be happy. I have ripped her from the light of Paradise, and she fears she will never return. Her existence is cold now, and she no longer possesses senses of touch, taste, or smell. She takes no pleasure in our reunion, so I take none, either.

She lies beside me at night, sometimes whispering to me, sometimes silent and refusing to answer me though plainly visible. Sometimes I neither see nor hear her, and only the painful chill in the air signifies her presence.

Yet, though her state is much diminished, I confess I could not bear to again be without her. She must remain here. I will find the keys to her happiness. I will open her spirit's heart and find again the great affection she had for me in life.

I set down the journal and magnifying glass and yawned, rubbing my eyes, the combined exhaustion of yesterday's long drive and the long night finally catching up with me. Tiredness, my old friend, was sometimes the only thing powerful enough to overpower the feelings of fear and anxiety that came with facing the restless dead, the memories of them clinging to you when you went home like psychological mud and filth from a bad day's work.

When I clicked off the lamp, sunlight seeped through a crack in the motel room's stained old curtains. I took one of the two plastic coat hangers from the closet and clamped the curtains together, creating more darkness.

Back on the bed, I pulled my sleeping bag around me and closed my eyes.

Instantly I saw the cadaverous face, the dark eye

sockets, the rotten old clothes, the skeletal hand reaching for me. The snarling German voice.

My eyes flew open, and suddenly I was grateful rather than annoyed for the corona of sunlight seeping around the window curtains. This is exactly why I didn't wear a sleeping mask like Stacey. I own one, because sometimes I just need it to sleep during the day, but I don't like it because I have frequent work-related nightmares, even between cases. It can be panic-inducing to open your eyes on solid darkness when you need the reassurance of light.

I sighed. Then I took a deep breath, imagined each part of my body relaxing, and slowly counted backwards from twenty to one, one number per long in-and-out breath.

The trick relaxed my mind, maybe not completely, but enough that I could slide down into a troubled sleep. I found myself lost in a maze of a library lit by black candles, with diseased-looking crows pecking at the old leather volumes and ripping the parchment inside, skulls watching me from the higher bookshelves, skeletal hands reaching out through the lower shelves to grab at my wrists and ankles.

I finally awoke in the early afternoon and decided I'd had enough bad dreams for one day.

A hot shower helped improve my mood, though the dismal motel shower with the weird splotch stains kept it from improving too much. I definitely wouldn't be soaking in this tub at any point, not even if the apocalypse happened and this was the only bath tub left on Earth.

"Wake up, sunshine." I gave Stacey a shake when I was ready. "We're visiting their graves today."

"Aw, no. A creepy old graveyard?"

"But first, the local courthouse and library to dig through property records and old newspapers on microfilm."

"Aw, can't we just skip to the creepy old graveyard?" Stacey yawned and reluctantly began to dress.

Chapter Eight

We stopped for a quick lunch at a place near the motel called Locos. I didn't expect much, but we'd struck some surprising gold, food-wise. My sandwich was a "Gobbler" with grilled turkey and bacon. Maybe I was just hungry, my appetite and mood restored after several hours at the cheap motel, which really emphasized how bad the emotional climate was at the old house in Philomath.

We checked out of the motel, not entirely sure our possessions would be safe while we were away working all night, and not really wanting to commit ourselves to another day's stay, either.

Soon we were chugging down the road in the van again, Athens behind us and a tree-lined highway ahead. East of Athens, for a long way, was a panorama of tiny historic towns, farmland, and protected forests pretty much all the way to the Savannah River, flowing toward home, where I personally would much rather have spent the night than the rundown motel.

The drive gave me plenty of time to catch Stacey up on my preliminary reading of the journal.

"Aw, he just wanted to summon the spirit of his poor wife, who died tragically," Stacey said. "It's like a Hallmark Channel movie. Well, maybe a Halloween one."

"It doesn't sound like it worked out for either of them," I said. "And I suspect he pulled something else through from the other side, too."

"Like the medieval jerk in the jerkin?"

"Exactly."

The Oglethorpe County Library was our first stop on the long road back to the late professor's mansion, a little brick building with four white columns topped by a triangular pediment.

"They really went for that ancient Greek stuff around here," Stacey said.

"See, this is the kind of library I like," I said, leading the way to the entrance. "Well-lit with no murderous ghosts lurking in the shadows."

"You're just assuming that," Stacey pointed out.

The public library was definitely pleasant and not scary at all, and more importantly, they had the local *Oglethorpe Echo* newspaper on microfilm going back to 1874. Dr. Marconi's recent obituary had been no trouble to find, but Piper had died decades earlier, before everything went digital.

Working for a private detective agency doesn't come with many perks—it's virtually perkless, to be honest—but I did have access to databases used by licensed investigators and law enforcement. They call it data fusion, and it's a little spooky how much they can pull together from public and semi-public records.

Soon I'd tracked down the key details about Piper's life, such as the date of her birth, marriage, and death.

Armed with that, I quickly found her obituary in the newspaper archives.

Pipette Overbrook Marconi, 26, was preceded in death by her father, Granton Overbrook. She is survived by her husband, Dr. Philip Marconi of Oglethorpe County, and her mother, Annalee Waldrum of Folkston, Georgia.

I double-checked my notes on Dr. Marconi. "Hey, Stacey?"

"Yes?" she asked from the other microfilm machine, sounding dead bored.

"Did you pick up that Dr. Marconi's wife was a few decades younger than him?"

"Didn't look that way in the painting."

"Maybe that's why the house has paintings instead of photographs," I said. "He didn't like the age difference being so obvious."

"Maybe. Weirdo. So I guess we're done here—"

"I'm going to dig back, see what else I can find."

"Ugh! Didn't you promise me a creepy old

graveyard?"

"If you're bored, you can head down to the courthouse and dig out the ownership history of that house and the land it's on. Find out everything you can about its past. See if you can find any sweet, sweet notices of construction or zoning variances."

"That is supposed to cure my boredom?"

"No, it's supposed to put you far enough away that I can't hear you complain." I checked the time on my phone, then handed her my keys. "Seriously, though, business hours are winding down, and I can't be in two places at once. Come back before the library closes at six."

"Fine," Stacey said, shuffling out with all the enthusiasm of a teenager on her way to do yard work.

I kept digging.

Piper's marriage announcement to Dr. Marconi described her as a "recent graduate of the University of Georgia with a Bachelor of Fine Arts in Dance" and her new husband "a distinguished professor of history."

There was no photograph of the happy couple. I guess the *Oglethorpe Echo* hadn't agreed to run a painting.

Dr. Marconi's file indicated that he'd been married before; Piper had been his second wife. His first had been named Vera.

In a 1973 newspaper, I found a public announcement for his book. Dr. Marconi, actually looking much as he did in the paintings at his home, stood in front of the metal arches at UGA's campus entrance, young and bearded and fairly handsome, his high-collared checkered suit and ascot looking very 1970s. Next to him stood a pretty young woman with long braids and bell-bottom pants, also looking very 1970s.

Associate professor Philip Marconi and wife Vera with his new book of Southern legends and folk tales.

The librarian apologetically interrupted my research and told me they were closing. Like most public libraries these days, they had to keep short hours.

I hurried outside, where Stacey was pulling into the parking lot. She waved, looking excited behind the wheel of the van, which made me wonder whether she really had spent the last couple of hours digging through property records at the courthouse.

"Guess what?" she said as I climbed into the van.

"You found a major break in the case."

"Huh? No. Guess what that courthouse has, though?"

"The identity of the medieval ghost guy?'

"No, you're not thinking. A clock tower! Just like the other town we passed through. Marty McFly would have no trouble getting back to the future from here."

"So this whole region could be thick with time travelers."

"Exactly."

"And did you get—"

"Yes, the boring property records. Some were so old and crumbly I couldn't stick them on the photocopier, but I took snapshots."

"Great. Any surprises?"

"Well, the house was originally built by a family named Taylor, which we knew, back in the year eighteen-forty-something-that-might-be-a-three-or-an-eight. The records are pretty faded, you can check for yourself. The sons fought on the Confederate side and never returned from the war. The lone heir was a daughter, who eventually sold the house and land to Lucio Marconi in 1878. After that, it's just inheritance within the Marconi family. Oh, and they expanded the house a couple of times. The biggest was adding those big back wings in the 1920s. Then some construction in the mid-80s, which seemed to be about converting those wings into that huge library. Taking out walls and floor all the way to the attic, replacing them with columns and beams and open space."

"And the county thought this was fine?"

"The county probably took a 'your property, your problem' approach. We're lucky they bothered requiring paperwork at all. It's pretty rural, not a lot of people, which means not a lot of government interference, probably. Philomath isn't even an official town. Most of the county's unincorporated."

"Yeah, sounds like you were busy at the courthouse."

"I also found the Marconi family graveyard," Stacey said. "It's on the property, way back from the house, but it looks like a path or small road runs to it. Based on an old hand drawing. Not sure how much we can trust that."

"Good. That's where I was planning to go next."

"Visit their graves and ask them nicely to stop haunting the house?"

"It couldn't hurt."

The sun was red and low behind us. Stacey flipped on the headlights and drove us into the darkness waiting ahead.

Chapter Nine

We turned off the main road, with all its fancy streetlights and painted lines and smooth blacktop, onto the bumpy, bouncy side road where the late professor's house was located, past the overgrown and forgotten fields.

The turn off to the cemetery lay beyond the house. It was easy to miss, so easy that we did miss it and had to back up slowly. Eventually we found the weedy dirt rut with tree limbs reaching in from both sides as if slowly trying to block the road, day by day and month by month.

"Should we walk?" Stacey whispered.

"Yeah, I don't think the van's suspension will make it through. We'd be bashing through trees, too."

We pulled onto the overgrown dirt track, just enough to get off the road. Limbs scratched at the van's roof. We definitely wouldn't be driving much farther.

We locked up the van, though I doubted any thieves would show up way out here. We probably could have left it parked in the middle of the road for hours without anybody noticing.

The path twisted slowly around the back of the old house, and we got a view of it through the trees at one point, lights on in the windows, Cherise and Aria at home. I'd texted Cherise to update her; we were expected in about an hour.

Not much moonlight penetrated the trees to illuminate the path. We drew on our heavy night vision goggles, which cast everything into eerie, otherworldly shades of green.

Branches and limbs littered the road, making it impassable for vehicles without investing a lot of labor first.

The woods were filled with rustling leaves and footsteps, things we couldn't see moving in the darkness around us.

A movement ahead, at the edge of the dirt road, made me tense up as something emerged onto the trail. Just a fox. He trotted across the road and out of sight.

A few minutes after that, another sound landed like a heavy boot in a pile of leaves beside me, but when I turned I saw nothing at all.

Animals, I told myself.

The dirt track led deeper into the woods.

It terminated at an iron gate. Beyond it lay the tall headstones of the Marconi family burial ground, enclosed by a high brick wall topped with sharp, pointy wrought iron. The gate had a forbidding, medieval appearance, like the entrance to a castle for the dead.

"What do you think?" Stacey whispered.

"Looks like bad place to get trapped," I said. "Let's hope those gates don't come creaking shut behind us once we're in there. It would be hard to climb out."

"I wish you hadn't said that." Stacey rattled the lock on the gate, then winced at the noise, as though worried it would attract unwanted attention from the cemetery's residents. "Maybe we should have asked Cherise if she has the key to this. Hey, we could maybe even go back now, get the key, make some hot chocolate, delay this as much as possible--"

"Are you getting cold feet?" I asked.

"Tell me this place isn't making your skin crawl," Stacey said, looking at the marble tombs. "My skin's crawling so much it feels like my jacket's full of bugs."

I took a deep breath. I did feel very uncomfortable about entering the graveyard, too, but I didn't want to add to her fear, so I went the brave-face route instead. "We'll be fine," I told her. "Let's just get it over with."

I brought out my lock-picking kit and went to work. The rusty gate lock resisted, but finally opened with a squeak of protest, like I'd annoyed a tiny guardian demon inside it.

"Is this a good idea?" Stacey asked as I pulled the gate open. "Couldn't we just be stirring them up?"

"The ones we're worried about are already stirred up." I stepped into the cemetery. The air felt cooler here, though maybe that feeling was just my emotional reaction to walking into the home of the dead.

A dozen tall headstones stood within, obelisks and pillars of granite and marble. The paved path continued out to a wide unused space that took up most of the room inside the cemetery wall, as though someone had expected the family to be fruitful and multiply over the generations. Weeds and scrubby pines inhabited that area.

Multiple generations of the family lay here, buried with progressively grander tombstones. The most recent and largest was a black marble obelisk engraved with the names of Philip Marconi and his wife Pipette. The professor's grave was recent enough that I could still discern the squares of grassy sod that had been placed over his burial site. The new grass was dead and yellow; it had died over the winter rather than taking hold.

Along with Dr. Marconi's name was an inscribed quote: *Knowledge is the wing wherewith we fly to heaven.*

His wife Piper—his second wife, apparently, which was an issue I really needed to research more deeply—lay beside him. Her name was also accompanied by an inscription: *To love beauty is to see light.*

"Get plenty of pictures of this," I said. "And the quotes, too. We need to figure out where they're from."

"That one's Shakespeare." Stacey pointed. "The knowledge one."

"Art school strikes again," I said. "And the other one?"

She shrugged, taking pictures. "Google will know."

I started recording audio using a digital recorder, its microphone roughly the size of a softball.

"Piper Overbrook Marconi," I said, stating the woman's name while looking at her grave. She had been a bit younger than me when she died, and already married for three years to a guy who was like fifty. A degree in dance, where I had one in psychology; she had studied beauty and movement while I'd focused on trying to understand the murky muck of the human mind. Similar ages, very different lives.

"I don't know much about you yet, but I'm beginning to learn," I continued. "I want you to know I'm here to help. I know you want to move on. You *can* move on. It's a choice you can make, I promise you, even if you can't see it now. If there's anything you want to say, you can tell us. We're listening."

Stacey and I remained quiet for a long moment. Maybe the big microphone was picking up something, some voice beyond the range of our hearing, maybe not. Later analysis would tell us.

"I read you died of a congenital heart failure. I'm sad to hear you died so young, Piper."

Pause. Silence.

"How did you feel about your husband? Did you love him? Were you happy with him? Or did you have regrets?"

A chilly wind creaked through the tree limbs in the overgrown, unused area of the cemetery.

"Are you still here, haunting the house?" I asked. "Do you feel trapped? Are you upset that your husband brought you back after your death, Piper?"

The tree limbs creaked louder in the wind, almost groaning. Dry leaves hissed across the ground. The cemetery darkened, clouds blotting out the scarce moonlight.

Something cold seemed to crawl up my back, and my heartbeat kicked up. I told myself not to panic.

We spent quite a while there, becoming increasingly spooked by the cold atmosphere and the endless whisper-level sounds in the darkness. Eventually we packed it in and headed back to the overgrown road, relieved to be out of the cemetery.

The walk back was colder. I kept glancing back, half-expecting to see a shape following us, maybe Piper or some other loose soul from the cemetery, or worse, the rotten medieval guy. I definitely didn't want him joining us out here in the woods.

I felt some relief as the path wound back toward the van, until Stacey hissed and jabbed me in the ribs. She pointed wordlessly through a break in the woods where we could see Marconi's house in the distance.

A new light had appeared, glowing softly inside an attic-level window at the back of the house. It was markedly different from the normal, yellowish room lights that illuminated some of the lower windows.

The light in the high window was bluish and cold, like it might cast a chill wherever it shone rather than any warmth.

It illuminated the shape of a girl, or perhaps a young woman, who gazed out the window as though watching us return from the cemetery.

Even at this distance, I could tell the pale face wasn't Cherise or Aria. I brought up my phone and zoomed in on the window, holding down the camera button so it would take a rapid burst of snapshots as I did.

By the time I zoomed in close, the girl and the cold blue light had vanished.

Stacey and I looked at each other, then raced up the dirt road toward the van, partly spooked by what we'd seen, but also in a hurry to investigate the part of the house where we'd glimpsed the strange girl.

Chapter Ten

Back at the house, we rushed to the library, Cherise and Aria trailing behind us down the first-floor hallway into the vast labyrinthine space of the main library.

I clambered up the nearest of the steep, narrow staircases, scaling it like a ladder. Stacey followed close behind.

"You really shouldn't go up there," Cherise called after us. She and Aria remained on the ground, both of them watching us skeptically.

"I know," I said. "I'd rather not be up here."

The second-story walkway was narrower and creakier than I would have liked. It had a railing, but clearly that hadn't stopped Dr. Marconi from falling to his death. I assumed it wouldn't keep me safe, either.

I walked past shelves of texts on psychology, sociology, and anthropology embossed with illustrious names like William James and Margaret Mead that gave me college flashbacks. There was no time to browse, though.

In the dim upper reaches of the library, Stacey reached for her holstered flashlight, but I touched her arm and shook my head. We couldn't keep chasing the ghosts off.

I brought out my Mel-Meter instead, tracking temperature and electromagnetic fluctuations as we moved.

Another steep, ladder-like staircase led us to the third level. The narrow walkway groaned under us and seemed to sway, though only slightly, enough that it could have been my imagination. The woodwork was decades old and I wasn't sure how well it had been maintained, or even how well it had been built in the first place. All I knew was that the railing wasn't reliable, the walkway was creaking, and it was a long drop to the floor below.

"I don't like it up here," Stacey whispered into my ear just behind me, her voice nearly making me jump. I was definitely jumpy.

We followed the walkway to a break in the bookshelves and stepped through to the other side. Ahead, beyond an intersecting wall of bookshelves, was the window where we'd spotted the girl.

I froze when we saw it.

"That's not good," Stacey said. "I mean, it has to

be bad, right?"

I didn't reply to her vague generalizations, because I was also at a loss for words. We both stared at the same thing—the broken handrail, a length of rope tied in place as a half-hearted gesture of repair.

"The girl in the window was standing right where he fell," I said, by way of stating what was obviously obvious.

Stacey and I stood there a moment, not sure what do with all the questions and possibilities this raised. Was Piper mourning the death of her husband? Or had she been the one who'd pushed him? Or was she trying to tell us something about how he'd died?

There was no sign of the apparition now, but maybe she was still present.

I advanced cautiously, holding out my EMF meter.

"This seems like a bad idea," Stacey whispered.

"Record this," I said.

She sighed and raised a video camera. "Why not? I can add this to my YouTube channel about stupid things to do in a haunted house."

I eased closer to the window and the broken railing, keeping my back flat against the bookshelves, as though creeping along a narrow ledge on the side of a building or high cliff. It certainly felt as precarious.

My EMF meter detected a spike in activity ahead.

"Piper, are you there?" I asked the empty space

in front of the window. "Did you hear us outside?"

No obvious response came. Stacey's hands trembled as she held the camera. She glanced through the broken railing to the floor far below, where Cherise and Aria watched us—from a safe distance, as though concerned we might fall and land on them.

I was feeling apprehensive, too, but I had to believe it was significant that Piper had showed herself to us right after we'd visited her grave. I just didn't know whether she was reaching out for help, or warning us, or threatening us.

"Do you have a message for us? We're listening." I spoke softly, gently, as though coaxing a frightened animal. I kind of hoped Cherise and Aria couldn't hear me from down on the ground floor as I tried to strike up a conversation with an invisible person, because I'm sure it sounded crazy. And they didn't need more of that in their lives. "Piper? Would you like to say something? Or show us something?"

There was a long silence. The walkway creaked, though neither Stacey nor I had moved.

"Is this where your husband died?" Pause. "How did he die?" Pause. "Do you miss him? Is that why you cry? What troubles you?" I was trying to think of emotional, evocative questions that might elicit a response. "What do you want? To move on? To return to the other side? Do you miss being there?"

I crept ever closer to the window. My EMF meter displayed stronger readings at every step, giving me hope that the entity was still there. There were no wires or outlets that I could see, nothing that might have given off misleading electrical readings. Lighting was meant to come from the chandelier a few meters away, and it was turned off.

"The inscription on your grave reads 'To love beauty is to see light.' What does that mean to you?" I asked.

"It's Victor Hugo," Stacey murmured, looking at her phone with one hand while recording me with the other. "The *Les Misérables* guy."

"We can help you leave this house," I said. "Don't you want to move on? Leave these people alone?"

When it seemed clear that we would have no repeat appearance from the girl in the window, I turned and started back along the walkway.

"We'll add a camera and microphone up here tonight," I said. "Let's head down and tell Cherise —"

All the lights on my EMF meter lit up as an unseen energy crackled the air around me. Suddenly I grew dizzy and disoriented, my senses distorting like I'd been jabbed with a needle full of nightmare-inducing hallucinogens.

The bookshelves and walkways and steep staircases suddenly made no sense, an elaborate Escher sculpture of a room with no clear up or down. My head spun. I wasn't sure where I was going, but I kept looking at that broken railing and thinking how I needed to get away from it.

I took a step, and then another, but it was all wrong because the broken railing grew closer, and I could see the long drop beyond, the tunnel of books and ladders spiraling down to the impossibly distant floor.

Unseen hands grabbed me.

I fell what seemed like the wrong way, but it must have been the right way, because I slammed into bookshelves instead of toppling through empty space.

One shelf dug painfully into my lower back; another cracked into the base of my skull. I wasn't falling, but I thought I might be crushed to death against those shelves full of books. *Ground into pulp fiction* was a thought that whirled through my confused brain.

Stacey was holding me, gripping my hand tight, shouting.

"Ellie, can you hear me? Ellie, snap out of it!"

And then, as if her words and touch were an incantation of some kind, I did snap out of it.

I slumped against the bookshelves, gripping Stacey's hand. A thick, almost waxy cold sweat coated my skin, as if my body was fighting a severe illness.

"Are you okay?" Stacey asked, her shift in tone indicating she'd noticed that I'd shifted back to normal, more or less.

"What happened?" I whispered.

"You, uh, wandered over to the railing like you were going to jump," Stacey said.

"We need to get out of here right now."

"Sure. There's your EMF meter." She pointed to where I'd dropped it on the walkway near the broken railing. "No, wait! I'll grab it! You just... walk that way. Stay tight to the bookshelves." Stacey was talking to me like I was demented, and I guess I had been, for a moment.

She walked with a hand on my shoulder, following close as I traveled the narrow walkways and climbed down steep stairs, finally reaching solid ground below.

"Everything okay?" Cherise asked; I couldn't tell whether her concern was for my well-being or over the possibility that I was a lunatic who'd somehow talked her into letting me wander her house at night. There was probably room for both concerns.

"Yes," I said, trying to look and sound professional despite my trembling knees and the outbreak of cold sweat. "We picked up some strong readings up there."

"You saw her standing where the old man fell and died?" Aria asked. "She pushed him, didn't she? The ghost killed him—"

"We don't know any of that for sure," I said, trying to calm her. It was strictly true but sounded a little hollow to me after what I'd just experienced. Maybe I'd glimpsed Dr. Marconi's final moments in life—confused, perhaps manipulated by an entity into walking right into his death like I'd almost done. "But your rule about nobody going up there is a solid one, because there's no way those rickety old walkways and ladders are safe. Unfortunately, we do need to stick some gear up there since it's an obvious haunting hotspot—"

"A hauntspot, we like to call those," Stacey chimed in, somewhat inaccurately, since only one of us prefers that term, and it's not me.

"—but we'll set it at a safe distance," I continued, railroading over Stacey's interruption.

"What exactly did you see again?" Cherise asked us.

"I took pictures." I brought out my phone and flipped through the 48 images I'd snapped in rapid succession. The first several were useless, showing the ground, the toe of my boot, a nearby tree.

Once they lined up on the window, they showed some hint of what I'd seen. The first pictures of the windows, when the camera was still zoomed out, showed a pale bluish glow and a hint of a figure standing within.

As the images zoomed in, the glow faded and vanished. Closer shots caught a couple of faint orbs in the window, which can indicate spirits, but can also be nothing but dust or water vapor. Maybe we'd find something interesting when we examined the orbs more closely on Stacey's computer, but the resolution was already pretty chunky on the extreme zoom-in.

The closest pictures showed nothing but a dark window. No glow, no face, no orbs.

"Did you get anything, Stacey?" I asked.

"No, the stupid camera was packed away and I didn't have time. That girl was just there and gone."

I nodded. "Aria, would you mind describing again the crying girl you saw in the hallway? Unless it upsets you—"

"Seeing it upsets me. Talking about it makes it a little better. It's people telling me *not* to talk about it that's upsetting." She scowled at her older sister.

"Enough," Cherise said. "I believe something unusual is happening. It's that or I have to think you're all crazy. As I said, maybe I haven't seen what y'all have seen, but I've had my share of strange moments in this house, too."

"Like what?" I asked, eager to get her to open up, to provide whatever insight she could into this house.

"Just working in the library late at night," she said. "All the old woodwork up there. It creaks. It groans. It's probably something to do with the humidity and temperature changes from day to night. The bookshelves are anchored in the supports that hold up the house." She pointed to some of the massive wooden columns. They were dark wood, not white like the portico columns out front, but otherwise they mirrored the shape and size of those front columns. There were actually more columns in here than out front. "Other times, I feel like I'm being watched, sometimes from above, or sometimes like there's someone behind me, looking over my shoulder while I read those creepy old books. But there's nobody there, it's just a feeling. And sometimes..." She glanced at her sister.

"Don't worry about me," Aria said. "I'm the one who's been telling *you* there's problems, remember?"

"Sometimes, I feel those drawings in the books are looking back at me," Cherise said, her voice dropping low as if reluctantly admitting to something shameful. "The strange masked people. The drawings of the risen dead. The contorted beasts, the monsters. The... demons." She covered her eyes and shook her head. "I can't keep doing this. I'm so drained."

"You think you're tired, try being me," Aria said.

"The loss of energy can be another sign of a haunting, too," I said. "Negative entities can feed on the living, and you may feel the drain physically, mentally, or emotionally."

"How about all of the above?" Cherise asked, smiling thinly, without much humor.

I nodded. "I recommend you let us stick around a while longer. I'll need to dig into Dr. Marconi's personal records as well as his research."

"His study should have all that." Cherise gestured toward the hallway where we'd passed the reading room and the study earlier. "Dig away, I don't care."

"It would be faster—and much cheaper—if we stay here on the property during our investigation," I said. "It's a long drive from home, and even cheap motels start to add up after a couple days."

"We could camp! There's tons of neat woods," Stacey said, as if we hadn't just suffered through a creepy walk to the cemetery through those supposedly neat woods. "We could bonfire, toast marshmallows, tell ghost stories—which Ellie and I know a lot of—"

"That really wasn't where I was going with this —" I began.

"If you're worried about whether I brought camping gear, fear not," Stacey said.

"It's just chilly at night—" I began, again.

"That's why we bonfire!"

"I don't believe 'bonfire' is a verb," Cherise said.

"Thank you!" I said. "Anyway, we have bunks built into our van, and we really only need to sleep during the day. It would just be nice, if it's not too much trouble, if we could stay out there." The van's accommodations were basically terrible, but not necessarily more terrible than our last motel room. Cleaner, too.

"Stay in the extra bedroom!" Aria said. "Your stuff's already there, and I need more people in this house. Especially ghost experts."

"That's us," Stacey said. "We can tell stories about the haunted hotel, the haunted corn maze, the haunted old mansion in Savannah, the other haunted old mansion in Savannah, or the other *other*—"

"I don't want to hear ghost stories. I want you to do your job and get rid of the ones we have," Aria said, coldly.

"Aria, don't speak to them like that," Cherise said. "You're welcome to stay in that spare room."

"Yes!" Aria said, quickly. "We need you here. I'll make you breakfast every day!"

"You will catch up on sleep," Cherise told her. "Now that they're here, you can rest and let someone else think about these things. You just think about school."

"How could I not?" She rolled her eyes. "It's the only thing you ever talk about."

"Because you can't afford to do poorly. Your middle school performance determines your placement in high school, and your performance there determines your college options, and what you do in college—"

"Blah blah determines the rest of my life, so if I screw up now I won't get buried in a fancy enough coffin when I'm dead," Aria said.

"Aria!"

"We should get to work." I nodded at Stacey, and we walked out to the van for more monitoring gear.

"Are you sure you're okay?" Stacey whispered to me outside. "What exactly happened up on the walkway?"

"I was completely disoriented. I could have sworn I was moving away from the broken railing, that I was specifically trying to walk away from it. Somehow my body did the exact opposite of that."

"So maybe something was oppressing you?" That's when ghosts get pushy and problematic, and maybe start to influence your behavior, but aren't quite possessing you. Yet.

I nodded. "I think you're right. Oppression. There was an energy surge, like the EMF meter detected the entity when it reached into my brain to scramble it up. Or whatever it did."

"And we're thinking it's probably the same entity that killed the professor?"

"I have to admit there are some fairly exact parallels between what happened to him and what happened to me." I looked at Stacey. "Thanks for saving me."

"Pfft. That's an exaggeration. Let's just try not to die on this case."

"Sounds like a good plan to me."

We headed back inside to prepare for our second night of observation, feeling more worried about our own safety than before. It can be a dangerous job; sometimes they're really out to get you.

Chapter Eleven

Reluctantly, we clambered up into the stairs and walkways of the "hanging garden of books" again, carrying cases of gear, but we stayed far back from the window and broken railing area, though along the same walkway.

While Stacey adjusted the thermal camera, I looked behind us at another book-lined wall spanned by more confusing walkways and ladder-like staircases.

The walkways converged below us, on the second floor, at a pair of heavy dark wooden doors that matched other pairs throughout the house.

"That must be the back entrance to the master suite," I said.

"Also known as Ghost Central Station, right?" Stacey said. "Where the girl always sees the ghosts coming and going."

I nodded. "Though I wonder whether they're really coming from the bedroom or just passing through it on the way from the library."

"Huh. Let's point a camera that way."

Soon we were done. Stacey sat in the nerve center upstairs, keeping watch over everything like a guardian angel with an Alabama accent, connected to me via headset so she could let me know if the house became active as the hour grew later.

She had a tendency to chat, though, so I kept the volume low while I did my research.

First priority was learning about the mysterious first wife. I sat at the desk in Marconi's study with my laptop, pulled up the P.I. database, and plugged in what I knew about Vera Marconi—her name, her spouse, the house in which I sat as a former address.

There she was. Birth, marriage, divorce. She was still alive, residing in Arkansas.

"Whoa," I said aloud.

"I know, right?" Stacey said, apparently thinking I'd been listening to her. "So I told Jacob, you don't wear a plaid tie with a plaid shirt, even as a joke, because visually it's just too painful—"

"Did you know they had a kid?"

"Huh? Who?"

"Marconi and his first wife, Vera. Their son is Victor Marconi, now forty-four years old. And yikes, multiple arrests. Writing bad checks. Um, and crystal meth, about ten years ago."

"Yikes," Stacey agreed.

"Still alive. His obituary didn't even mention a son. Maybe they were estranged."

"That's sad."

I poked around, sifting through bits and pieces of the late professor's family history, trying to see if anything might shed light on this apparent haunting by his second wife and some other entity.

His antique wooden filing cabinets held his personal papers, portions of which were fairly organized, but a lot of loose papers were crammed in at random, sometimes crumpled up and jammed in between file folders—bills, bank statements, and other items dated in no particular order over the past ten years or so, as if he'd grown increasingly disorganized with age.

One thick folder held the paperwork about Piper's medical problems. I read through bits and pieces of it. A congenital heart defect had gone undetected until her heart began beating irregularly in her mid-twenties. They'd monitored the condition closely, but ultimately there was nothing to be done, and her death came soon after her diagnosis.

The professor's financial records were murky— maybe Jacob could help us clarify them—but it appeared he owned scattered real estate in a few towns, largely Athens and Augusta, from which he received rental revenue. He'd inherited a portfolio of stocks and bonds that had diminished significantly over the years, maybe from the expensive renovations and his own spending on his collection of obscure texts and artifacts.

Footsteps echoed out in the library, and I stiffened up, wondering if one of the ghosts was walking near.

"Ellie?" A voice asked behind me, and I jumped a little. I turned to see Cherise. "I didn't mean to startle you."

"I'm fine. Just jumpy. Is everything okay?"

"I found something. It might relate to that German voice you recorded."

"Oh, great." I stood and stretched. "Not that I wasn't having a fun and fulfilling time reading through insurance records. What did you find?"

She led me out of the study to the western part of the library, where she unlocked and rolled aside the door to the Tomb Room. Which, I assume, is not what Dr. Marconi had actually called it.

The darkness and heaviness of the room assaulted me almost immediately. I could smell old incense and smoke, and the sealed windows meant none of that had ever escaped. I tried to keep my eyes on Cherise and not the dusty cases of bones and or the brutal Aztec-looking statue with a head like a jaguar skull with a snake's tongue.

"This was sitting out on the desk, which is one of the clearest spots in the room. I think the items on his desk might have been things he was actively using. As opposed to the heaps." She gestured at the precarious piles all around. The second and third story shelves above us were just as chaotic and unorganized.

I followed her to an open book on the desk, then recoiled at the sight of a snake tail winding across the page, its tip curled in a small loop on the dried parchment.

"Is that... alive?" I asked, feeling stupid as I heard myself ask the question.

Cherise smiled thinly. "It's the bookmark."

I moved closer. The snake tail was dried and mostly flattened, long dead. I felt a little queasy as I reached out and touched it. It was sewn into the book's spine like a ribbon marker. The whole book was bound in dry, scaly leather. "Is this reptile hide?" I asked.

"If it's not, it's certainly meant to look that way," Cherise said. "I found it open to that page."

Grimacing, I eased aside the dried snake-tail bookmark, trying not to break it.

The text was hand-written in densely packed German. I couldn't read it, but the hand-drawn image was gruesome enough. One showed a skeleton on a table or altar, partially wrapped in bits of cloth. Candles burned in its eye sockets. Strange symbols were drawn all over the table where it lay. Another image showed a crazed-looking man cutting his own wrist, the blood dripping into a chalice.

"I can't say I like the looks of this," I said, my stomach feeling tight and cold. "What does the text say?"

"Supposedly, these are rituals for raising the dead, and for banishing them again."

"Raising them how? As spirits or, you know, zombies?"

"It doesn't use terms like that. It does make a distinction between three kinds of souls: fallen, ascended, and wandering. Each requires a different kind of ritual."

"Do we know the title of this book? Or author?"

Leaving the bookmark in place, she carefully shifted the dried, oversized pages forward. She was clearly adept at handling fragile, crumbling texts.

The first page in the book was illustrated with a three-headed serpent surrounded by text.

"These are curses," Cherise explained. "Instead of invoking a muse, it calls upon 'spirits of the infernal realms.' He tells us dark spirits are bound to the book. He also warns that trafficking in dark arts can cost one's soul, for... he writes, 'Souls are the coin of the underworld.' And finally his name is signed here." She pointed to the bottom of the page.

I read it aloud: "Johann Gremel."

"He calls himself an 'ordained enchanter of the hidden school.' Does that mean anything to you?"

I shook my head. "I'll check this against Dr. Marconi's personal journal and see what he says. This fits with something he wrote about Piper—that he summoned her down from Paradise, and her ghost seemed sad."

"Imagine that," Cherise said. "You make it all the way to heaven, only to be hauled back down to Earth to live as a ghost. Well, not exactly 'live'..."

"That's what he wrote. That was why she was so sad, he thought."

"So what did he do about it?"

"I'll let you know when I read that far. It should be more interesting than the property records at the courthouse."

"Algebra worksheets are more interesting than those," Stacey grumbled in my ear, and I turned down the volume on my headset again.

"Looks like I'll be down here for a while. I'll grab my laptop bag. Do you mind if we prop this door open?" I didn't like the idea of the Tomb Room door being able to roll shut and trap me inside.

We lugged over one of the room's sturdy wooden chairs, which had leather backs and seats that somehow didn't make them any more comfortable, and propped open the Tomb Room's bookshelf door. It would now be a tight squeeze getting in and out, but at least I wouldn't find myself trapped inside.

I grabbed my laptop bag from the study and brought out the late professor's journal. I settled down in the chair at the Tomb Room desk, the awful illustrations facing me. Wall sconces lit the room, but sputtered like dying candles. A chandelier hung high above us, beyond the ladders and walkways and upper bookshelves of the room.

"It doesn't work," Cherise said. "None of the chandeliers work. Maybe they've been shut down at the fuse box. I didn't go trying to fix them."

"Well, I won't start any electrical fires trying to figure it out, either," I said.

"I'll be down here working for a while, too," she said. "I don't like working at night in here, but I don't have much choice because of the deadline."

"Great. I'm not eager to be alone in here, either."

I flipped through the professor's journal in

search of Gremel's name.

The earliest mention was among a number of books Marconi had acquired on a collecting tour of Europe about twenty years earlier. He'd purchased any occult text he could find, searching for ways to contact the dead.

I had to read again about how he ached from the loss of his wife, how he longed with all his being to reach her somehow, even if the contact was only slight and fleeting.

It felt a bit different to read this knowing that he'd had a previous wife and a son somewhere who he never mentioned, that he'd met Piper when he was approaching fifty; she was an undergraduate, and his own son was elementary age. Maybe he'd used some form of dark magic on her, or maybe she'd been overwhelmed by his influence and authority, or dazzled by his big mansion in the country. Maybe I was just being a little judgy of others, but I guess I couldn't help feeling that as I read it.

I wondered whether Piper had come to regret her choice. Maybe her medical problems had arisen and ended her life too quickly for that.

I also had to note the possibility that a supernatural presence had already existed in the house before they were married. Maybe the young girl's heart problems, which had somehow gone undetected while she earned a degree in dance, actually stemmed from life in a haunted house.

But one problem with that hypothesis was that Vera had lived there for more than a decade without such issues. She and her son Victor were still alive today.

Heck, maybe Vera had put a curse on Piper as revenge. That was just a random thought; I had no evidence that Vera was into such things, or that such things actually worked, anyway. But I had encountered some who could bind spirits and then use them to attack others—well, those were ancient Phoenicians who had now been dead for millennia themselves, but surely others could do it, too.

Marconi wrote, quite a bit later, that the rituals described in Gremel's book finally allowed him to draw Piper's soul into his house.

I begin tonight with the rites for recalling an ascended soul, Marconi wrote, *for a being of such innocence and rare beauty as Piper could surely never be condemned among the fallen. Should this fail, I shall instead follow the formulae for evoking a wandering spirit, for perhaps she wanders, her soul's heart broken at our separation from one another, just as her body's heart was broken in life.*

My eyes rolled a little at his presumption that she would be spending the afterlife pining for him. It sounded like he was projecting a bit. Then again, I hadn't really known either of them, so I didn't know how they'd felt.

His preparations for the ritual included bathing, fasting, and other topics I skimmed past until I found where he recounted the actual ritual:

...after the burning of incense and offerings, after the incantations and the spilling of my blood, I saw her dimly. At first, she appeared only as a reflection in the black crystal, a faint image of her gazing at me from beyond. I felt her

presence in the room, a rising energy like the crackling air of an electrical storm.

More blood I offered, cutting myself with the knife of gold and ivory that took such effort to obtain, spilling it into the golden chalice for her golden soul; I know not whether the blood truly gives sustenance to the spirit, as Gremel wrote in his instructions for the rite, or whether the shedding of blood is of symbolic or energetic importance instead.

It matters not; the more I gave, the stronger she became.

Soon I heard her voice—soft, so soft it was nearly drowned by the low hissing burn of the incense and candle flame—but it was she.

"Who calls me?" her voice whispered, and it sounded true, though her words were stiff and formal. I reminded myself she was a spirit now, and her years in the land of the dead had likely changed her, perhaps profoundly. It matters not to me, so long as she has returned. "Who brings me here?" she asked.

"It is me, my love," I said. "I have given all to bring us together again. Every day apart from you has been like a chasm of inescapable misery—"

"Did you really say that out loud?" I asked.

"Sorry?" Cherise looked up from where she was working across the room. I'd pretty much forgotten she was there, otherwise I would not have been talking to myself.

"Uh, nothing," I said. "I found the part where he summoned her."

I read ahead, through Marconi's joy at Piper's return, even in her insubstantial ghost form.

As I'd already seen in my skimming, though, things turned sour. She was permanently sad, despite his desperate attempts to cheer her up, to make their reunion a happy one.

I have placed her favorite flowers, delicate boat orchids, in every room and endeavored to keep them thriving, though our climate is too hot. I have written her verses describing my love, a love that spans the worlds of life and death. I play her beloved records, Debussy and Auric and Bartok.

Yet she draws no pleasure, but weeps, or is silent. Sometimes days pass and I do not see her but only sense her presence like a sad chill; I wish only for her happiness.

Her only comfort seems to be when I suffer for her, drawing my blood with the knife to signal my continued devotion. I bleed into the goblet, and she favors me by appearing in full flesh, wearing only gauzy raiment like clouds, or nothing at all, for she is pure. Then she smiles, and I feel a sense of her delight in the air.

At times these manifestations cause me to boil with desire, but there is no satiation, for her body is sometimes restored to its beauty but never its substance. She is like the clouds and the stars, celestial and untouchable.

Did my eyes roll yet again? Maybe.

Pages of desperation and despair followed, descriptions of her intermittent apparitions and her ice-cold presence beside him in bed.

"I'm off to sleep," Cherise told me. "I hope I don't dream about this stuff. I hope you don't, either."

I wished her good night and resumed focusing on the journal.

Though my love has returned, the pain of loss is only sharpened and renewed, for we cannot touch, and only rarely speak. She is stiff and distant with me then; our old intimacy is gone, buried with her in the grave.

Misery grows like a tumor inside me. I long to make her whole again, like Eurydice when her beloved Orpheus brought her out of the underworld—then foolishly lost her before reaching the world of the living.

Should I have the chance, I will not repeat the mythical musician's grave error.

I squinted. Was he making a pun with the *grave error* bit? Or was he too somber and serious to even realize it?

And, much later, his handwriting almost too cramped and spidery to read despite the magnifying glass, he wrote:

I have failed again. Another attempt that seemed worthy —for a moment she appeared whole, and I touched her. She was soft and damp, warm but cooling quickly. I knew it was temporary, made from the blood and scales of sacrificed reptiles, the black ichor of crushed insects, the innards of strange fish from distant waters. I had collected and mixed these myself in the bath tub, along with the prescribed minerals and incantations, the promises of servitude to the Great Fallen Spirits.

For this, I had the momentary pleasure of touching her as she rose from the bath of dark fluids, her skin and hair, the surface of her, forming a lifelike illusion. Her skin was spongy, and I knew her to be hollow within; but how I delighted to touch her again regardless.

"I have come for you," she said, and for once she was not crying. For once she was not a sad echo of her former self, but blazingly alive, her blonde hair red with animal blood and hanging in wet ropes all over her face and shoulders. Her blue eyes glowed in that perfect face; even with the blood and filth

that coated her, I could discern the high cheekbones and full lips, all the features that had drawn me so powerfully and hopelessly to her when we met.

"But you were probably still married when you met," I murmured. The date of his marriage to Piper was less than a year from his divorce from Vera.

I saw then that all miracles are possible.

"I love you," I told her, and embraced her. Her arms encircled my neck, her soft lips pressed against mine. I felt her lithe dancer's body against my aged and decrepit one, and I was alive and felt excitement as I had not in so many years. So many years of searching for her, reaching for her, craving this moment again, her flesh against mine again.

Her touch was not quite as it had been in life—in this form, she had no bones, no true core, simply animal parts brushed over her spirit like warm paint, giving her texture and color. She was dripping wet, and none of it was water.

Then she was gone.

Our kiss ended, and I opened my eyes. I was still wet from my face down to my feet, moist with the blood and innards of nineteen animal species. Where the tip of her tongue had slipped between my lips, I removed the crushed black shell of a palmetto bug.

The conjuring had ended in moments, after weeks of exacting preparation.

I had lost her again.

I knelt before the foul soup of decay filling the bathtub and wept.

This is not enough.

I must find a way to make her flesh again.

The next few pages detailed more occult

research, more disappointments in his attempts at necromancy.

The final page offered only a few quickly scrawled lines:

I have failed. There is no path forward. The rest of my miserable years shall be spent without more than a ghost of her, until I finally lose my form and join her.
The only hope of true reunion lies in my death.

I reread those lines a few times. Was there a chance Dr. Marconi had killed himself?

Ragged little ridges of paper were visible just ahead of this final page. I ran my finger down the middle of the book.

Someone had torn out pages here.

Dr. Marconi himself? Cherise, who had the thick ring of house keys with the desk key? Some unknown third party with secrets to hide?

Whatever it was, I was missing some part of what he'd done in his further attempts to resurrect his dead wife—an important part, most likely, because someone had gone to the trouble of striking it from an already fairly grisly record.

I checked the hidden cavity in the desk, but there were no loose pages in there. The golden-handled ivory dagger and golden chalice were; I pictured the elderly man puncturing himself, bleeding into the chalice for the sake of summoning his wife's ghost down from above.

It was hard to picture clearly, though, because there weren't many recent photos of Marconi available. Just those paintings of himself and Piper, of which I'd counted five around the house.

Having finished the journal, I squeezed past the propped-open door and the clutter around it and strolled through the main part of the library. I looked up at the broken railing, but there was no sign of the pale ghost girl.

"Stacey, any updates?" I whispered over the headset. I didn't want to run off any ghosts who might have been thinking about manifesting. Besides, the quiet library environment almost compelled me to keep my voice down, as though some irritable librarian would emerge to shush me.

"We have some indicators ticking in the upstairs hall again. No clear cold spot now, but overall temp is down compared to the rest of the house. The EMF meters are registering activity, but I'm not seeing or hearing anything. Cherise went to her room a while ago. How's it going down there?"

"I finished his journal. We also found one of the old necromancy texts he was using. Written in German by a guy named Johann Gremel."

"Could he be our angry German in the jerkin?" she asked.

"If his ghost is somehow attached to his book, then yes," I said. "But there's no reason for him to be territorial about the house."

"Unless he's decided he likes it here," Stacey said. "Do we know how long he's been here?"

"His grimoire has been here for a couple of decades. Marconi acquired it at an estate sale in Bavaria."

"So maybe he's claimed the house for his own. Killed the owner for it. Maybe he's a super book dork like you and wants to haunt that library forever."

"There's definitely a lot of maybes at this point. The flip side: maybe he's just trying to warn us. And Aria. Maybe he's just being a helpful Harry in all this, and we're focusing on the wrong ghost because he looks scary."

"A scary Harry, yeah," Stacey mused. "So you're thinking Piper might be the dangerous ghost? Maybe she grew to hate old Professor Marconi after their marriage, and came back as a ghost to shove him off that balcony."

"Or maybe Gremel killed Marconi, and Piper's weeping because of it," I said. "And here's what's behind door number three: Marconi could have been suicidal." I caught her up on the salient points of his journal.

"He summoned her into a goop of bug guts and lizard blood?" Stacey gasped after I recounted the gross parts.

"And fish organs," I reminded her.

"That is... *not* romantic. Never mind Hallmark Channel Halloween. It's more like Hallmark Channel Chainsaw Massacre."

"So a lot of this comes down to what Marconi was doing in his final years, and most importantly those last days of his life. It sounds like he was mainly a hermit. Who had contact with him? There's Cherise, and whatever mutual contact landed her the job. Piper's mother is still alive, too. Maybe she was in touch with him—"

"Ellie, we have activity upstairs," Stacey interrupted. "The cold spot's back, and moving fast."

Chapter Twelve

"Did the cold spot emerge from the master suite into the upstairs hall again?" I looked up toward the closed set of dark doors on the second floor, the rear entry to the master suite.

"That's a big yep."

I decided to take a shortcut and also have a look, finally, at what lay within the master suite area. Cherise was reluctant to let us investigate that portion of the late professor's home, but it seemed critical to me.

I climbed the creaky staircase to the second-story walkway, using my hands on the stairs in front of me; the staircase was nearly as narrow and steep as a ladder.

Approaching the dark doors to the master suite, I drew out my set of lock picks again.

I didn't need them. The doors weren't locked on this side. They were heavy, though, and it took some effort for me to pull one open.

The space beyond was pitch black. I clicked on my flashlight and turned it to its dimmest setting before entering.

It was a continuation of the upstairs front hallway. It had probably all been a single upstairs hall at one point, but later walled in to create a private lair.

The rooms were cold; my Mel-Meter confirmed it, along with elevated electromagnetic readings.

Actual photographs, not paintings, hung on the walls here. Some featured Marconi at faculty and university functions in decades past; he had one picture with a chubby silver-haired guy who, I'm pretty sure, was the state governor when I was a kid, but the picture wasn't labeled. There were also a couple of framed newspaper and magazine articles related to his book on Southern lore.

The opposite side of the hall featured pictures of Piper, performing in a variety of irregular avant garde costumes, lots of modern dance kinds of stuff that I really don't know about, but it definitely looked hard and uncomfortable, her body contorting into strange shapes.

The pictures spanned back to her childhood, showing her as a young girl dressed as a tiny ballerina, or tap dancing in sparkling clothes, or wearing heavy makeup in beauty pageants. She'd apparently won Miss Okefenokee twice, at the Little Miss levels and later the Teen level.

There were even actual pictures of the couple from their wedding, Dr. Marconi looking distinguished and gray, not the youthful version of his face looking out from the portraits around his home.

I saw no pictures of the late professor's ex-wife, which wasn't shocking given that he'd remarried, but there were also no pictures of his son Victor, not at any age. Dr. Marconi showed more interest in his second wife's childhood than his son's.

"I'm upstairs," I whispered to Stacey over my headset.

"Cold spot is doing that hesitating-in-the-hallway thing again. I hate when the ghosts go still like that. Come on, *do* something, cold spot. Be a good spot."

"Anything on night vision?"

"Not a thing."

"Keep me posted."

I explored cautiously along the hallway, finding a sizable linen closet, then a bathroom with a large dark marble tub. I wondered if that was the same tub Marconi had filled with animal parts and blood for his unsatisfying summoning. The stain-splotched tub back at our cheap motel suddenly grew more appealing by comparison.

Another door opened onto a large bedroom, the king-sized bed shrouded with dark curtains like a stage; I almost expected the curtains to part, revealing actors or marionettes inside. A couple of chairs offered a sitting area by the bedroom's fireplace, surrounded by more bookshelves. Another painting of Professor Marconi and Piper hung above the fireplace. The windows were shuttered, keeping the room in deep shadow.

My EMF meter indicated elevated activity in here, and I felt more than a little unsettled, as though I wasn't alone in the room, though I saw no one. Perhaps the old bedroom was Piper's ghostly lair, the place from which she emerged, weeping, late at night.

Or perhaps her lair was the next room, the last one in the private suite, a dance studio with golden-hued hardwood floors and mirrored walls. A big stereo cabinet with a record player and cassette slots stood in one corner, a 1980s relic that had probably been high end in its day, suitable only for vinyl-loving hipsters in our modern world. A huge selection of records and cassettes occupied its shelves. One end of the room had bookcases with volumes on dance and music.

A layer of dust coated everything, indicating the room hadn't been touched in decades.

I imagined Piper here, her golden hair tied back in a sweaty ponytail as she practiced, utterly unaware that her heart would soon blow out. I wondered how that had been discovered, and exactly where she'd died—here in the house? Or in a hospital?

The entire suite was kept permanently dark, the windows shuttered tight in every room.

"Ellie, it's getting colder, and it's moving," Stacey whispered.

"Toward Aria's room again?" I stepped toward

the dark doors dividing this master suite hallway from the guest hallway out front.

"No. Cherise's." Stacey took a breath. "Ellie, it just passed through Cherise's door. It's not in the hall anymore. It's in the room with her."

I shivered, not liking the sound of that.

It took some effort to unlock and heave open one of the pair of heavy dark doors that led from the front of the master suite into the upstairs hall.

"A strange new presence has emerged from the dark doors," Stacey intoned over my headset as I stepped out of those doors into the hall where our cameras watched. "Female. I can see her on night vision. On the thermal, she's red hot, one of the hottest ghosts I've ever seen."

"Well, thanks." I looked at Cherise's door, uncertain what to do. If it had been Aria, I would have knocked immediately, because she'd been reporting serious trouble with the ghosts.

Cherise, though, hadn't really wanted us here at all and was only allowing us to investigate for her little sister's peace of mind. She'd been insistent that we stay out of her personal space, which was generally reasonable but now seemed risky. What was the entity doing in her room? And which entity was it?

I leaned close to the door, feeling a little icky about trying to eavesdrop. There was nothing to hear, anyway.

Stacey spoke up just as the hallway grew colder and my skin began to crawl.

"Ellie...behind you."

I turned.

The cadaver man was there again, his shadowy, skeletal face staring at me from hollow sockets, his rotten cape draped over his rotten jerkin.

Having glimpsed him before, I managed to hold in a scream and resisted the urge to reach for my light. I had loaded up some Deep South Gospel music on my iPod Touch, too, which had seemed my best bet for evil-repelling music when going into an old plantation house. For Baron von Jerkin, though, I would have probably gone with something a little more medieval.

I held still, avoiding any sudden moves, silently regarding the dead thing before me and generally trying to act like it was a nervous horse I didn't want to scare off, while my own nerves were quite rationally screaming at me to run away.

It started to reach toward me again, which didn't help, but I held my ground even as its bony fingers moved toward my face.

"Johann Gremel?" I asked.

His movement paused. For a moment the shadows on his face grew thicker over his bones, like skin growing back. Dark, round shapes moved in the eye sockets, the suggestion of eyes.

"Why did you tell me to leave?" I asked.

Gremel—assuming that was his name—resumed reaching his hand. He extended one bony finger, almost like he meant to gouge me in the eye.

Then he pointed past me, at the closed door to Cherise's room.

"Is there another spirit in there?" I asked,

wondering if he even knew English, not that it always matters when dealing with the dead. Most of the time they aren't listening, anyway. "Is it Piper? Or someone else?"

If he heard my questions, he didn't respond. He kept pointing, not moving at all. The dead, when they manifest, have an eerie stillness. They lack all the little movements of the living—breathing, slight movements while shifting one's balance, fingers twitching and tapping.

Gremel stood like a gruesome statue, pointing his finger at the door as if he had nothing else to do for all eternity.

I turned sideways, looking at the door but definitely not wanting to turn my back to the ghost. I knew Stacey was watching out for me, but she was also hanging back, being professional and silent to avoid chasing away the ghost.

Apparently the apparition was just going to keep pointing, like the ghost of Christmas Future showing the way to my lonely grave, so I had little choice but to go ahead and check on Cherise.

I knocked on her door, hoping she was okay and that she wouldn't get angry and throw us out of her house. Also hoping the entity inside wasn't presenting a serious danger, to her or to me.

No answer came.

I knocked again, louder. "Cherise? Hey, I'm really sorry to bother you. Cherise?"

Still no response. I kept looking at Gremel, and he kept pointing.

"Fine, fine." I muttered, and I tested the

doorknob.

It turned, and the door opened.

Cherise lay in a four-poster bed that matched the antique wardrobe and dresser; it was my first glimpse of the room where she stayed.

She was deeply, solidly asleep, dressed in checkered flannel pajamas, arms and legs splayed out, snoring softly. Moonlight crept into the room from the window.

A strange black cloud with an oily surface, vaguely shaped like a person, hovered above Cherise as she slept.

It was the posture of a predatory entity preying on the living. If the black cloud was Piper, she'd certainly evolved into something very different since her death a few decades back.

I turned on my and twisted its head into floodlight mode, soaking the shadowy entity in all the white light I could summon.

In the surge of light, I could see something like an oily tentacle connecting the shape to Cherise's face. Feeding on her. Sucking the life out of her.

"Cherise!" I turned on the room's overhead light. "Stacey, come!"

With the lights on, the dark oil-cloud shape had vanished, but Cherise didn't respond to my shouting. She wasn't moving at all.

I ran to her and gave her a shake; she was as unresponsive as a rag doll. I checked her pulse, feeling my own rise in panic. She was alive, thankfully, but her pulse was low and faint.

I shouted her name again.

"What's up?" Stacey barged in, swinging her own

light around. "You okay?"

"She's not waking up," I said, shaking Cherise. "Something was in here, feeding on her, and now she's not waking up—"

"I'm up, I'm up," Cherise moaned softly, covering her closed eyes against all the light.

"What's everyone yelling about?" Aria rushed in, still dressed in her school clothes despite the late hour, clearly wide awake.

"We saw something," I said. "We followed an entity into your sister's room."

"Why are you in my room?" Cherise asked, anger creeping into her voice as she looked at me between her fingers. "I never wanted you in my *home*. You can't be in here!"

"I am so sorry, Cherise," I said. "But an entity came into your room. I saw it, and I think it could be very dangerous—"

"Enough! Get out of here. All of you." She waved at us, sounding furious and exhausted at the same time. "Turn that light off. I have work tomorrow."

I turned off the overhead as well as my flashlight, and nodded at Stacey to turn off hers. The dark cloud didn't return, though that didn't necessarily mean the entity was gone. Aria had turned on the hallway lights, so we weren't plunged into darkness. I didn't leave the bedroom, though; I was extremely reluctant after what I'd just seen.

"I'm sorry," I said again. "I was worried about you."

"What did you see?" Aria asked me.

"An entity came into this room." I held back on details, since they would only frighten her more. "I followed it."

"Was it the crying girl? Or the jerkin guy?"

"The jerkin guy was the one who insisted I check on her. Did either of you see him in the hall?"

Stacey and Aria looked into the hall, then at each other, then back at me, and shook their heads.

"Why are you still in my room?" Cherise groaned.

"So it was the crying girl?" Aria asked again, understandably pressing the issue.

"I didn't see a girl. What I saw was more of a dark cloud."

"What does that mean?" Aria asked.

"It means you should all *get out of my room!*" Cherise drew a pillow over her head.

"Cherise, can you remember what you were dreaming about?" I asked. "Did you have any nightmares?"

"No. I was having a really nice sleep and perfectly fine dreams until I woke up to this nightmare of you people still *not leaving my room.*"

"Okay, if you really want us to go—" I began.

"*Yes.* That's the underlying subtext here," Cherise said.

"We can talk in the morning." I nodded at Stacey and we hurried out to the hall.

"Is it really safe to leave her alone in there?" Aria asked.

"She was pretty insistent," I said. "So there's not much we can do. Maybe the entity will lie low the rest of the night, after all this attention from the living."

"Maybe I should stay with her tonight." Aria stared at the door in concern.

I didn't want her to do that, precisely because of the entity I'd seen. I would have preferred for Cherise to leave that room for the night, too, but we'd strayed perilously close to getting thrown off the case altogether.

"That could scramble our investigation," I said. "We need everything to be as normal as possible."

"Normal? In this house?" Aria shook her head and returned to her room, but I doubted she would sleep.

Chapter Thirteen

I stayed in the spare bedroom with Stacey the rest of the night, watching for any evidence of the dark cloud's return, though of course we wouldn't see it if the thing had simply lingered in Cherise's room. It could be in there, feeding on her now, and I was helpless to stop it or even to go back in there without angering Cherise.

This frustration kept me pacing up and down the bedroom floor, restless and worried.

"Don't you have something boring to read?" Stacey finally asked, clearly annoyed at my constant nervous motion.

"Plenty." I forced myself to sit down and review the material I had—Marconi's journal, the investigator database information about the professor and his family members: his ex-wife Vera, his estranged son Victor with the criminal record, his second wife Piper.

Piper's mother, Annalee Waldrum, was a veteran of four divorces and lived in the small town of Folkston, more than two hundred miles south of us. It was even south of our hometown, Savannah. Any farther south and Piper would have been a Florida girl instead of a Georgia one.

Annalee's marital history complicated her legal and economic ones. There was much bad credit, a repossessed car, an eviction from a duplex. She'd lived in several towns scattered across south Georgia and north Florida, but seemed to have settled back in Folkston in recent years.

Piper's childhood was becoming clearer—absent father, a mother who was present but not necessarily providing a stable environment. A weird tangle of beauty pageants and poverty, an extreme emphasis on the young girl's appearance and ability to perform for others.

Not long before sunrise, I met with Cherise down at the kitchen table.

"We have to piece together their last known mental states as best we can," I told her. She was still groggy as she drank her coffee at the kitchen table, still clearly annoyed at us for barging into her room the night before. "When you worked with Dr. Marconi, did he seem depressed to you?"

"I'm not sure I'm qualified to diagnose that," Cherise replied. "He didn't seem happy. He seemed mostly tired. He was pretty brusque with me, to be honest—all about the work, not a lot of pleasantries. But if he was emotionally troubled, he didn't discuss it. Mostly he laid out instructions and watched quietly while I worked. After a few days, he stopped bothering to watch and just reviewed my work before I left. Even then, he just grunted. The only sign he was happy with me was that he didn't fire me. If I didn't come for a few days, he would call to make sure I was still coming back. The schedule was pretty loose."

"How exactly did you end up with the job again?"

"A professor in the history department told me about it."

"Do you think we could speak with him?" I asked. "He may have been one of the last people to speak with Dr. Marconi. Maybe the only one who might be able to give some insight into his mental state and what his concerns were near the end of his life."

"I could ask, but..." She shifted and looked out the window, appearing uncomfortable. "I'm not sure how to say who you are and why you're involved. I'm sorry. I realize you take your work seriously, but it will sound strange to him. Dr. Anderson is an older, no-nonsense kind of guy. And he's on my dissertation committee. I don't want him to think I'm..." Cherise made a vague gesture so she didn't have to say *stupid* or *naive* or *superstitious* or *totally nutty*.

"I understand," I said. "We are a licensed private investigation firm. I could frame it as though we're doing a brief overview on behalf of the professor's estate. Tying up questions about his death and his property."

"Wouldn't that be dishonest?"

"I'm equally happy to tell him I'm investigating paranormal entities for you in the late professor's home."

"Let's go with the first thing."

"Okay. I plan to contact his surviving family members, too, but given their relationship—or lack of one—I'm not hoping for much. None of them live nearby, and it's usually easier to get them to open up in person."

"Did we see any more ghosts last night?" Aria entered the room dressed for school, backpack on her shoulder, and poured herself a large mug of coffee, to which she added much milk and sugar.

"You're drinking too much coffee for your age," Cherise said.

"Get the ghosts out of this house, or *us* out of this house, and I'll stop."

"You know I can't quit," Cherise said.

"That's how I feel about this coffee." Aria took a long, noisy slurp.

"We both need me to have this job. We have to survive."

Aria snorted. "So much for the amazing value of your fancy college degree." Then she headed out into the pre-dawn darkness, carrying the steaming mug with her. The bus arrived a minute later, covered in blinking and flashing lights, like a UFO arriving before sunrise to whisk her off to Planet

Middle School.

"I don't blame her," Cherise said quietly. "I'm starting to doubt this was the right choice, too."

"I want to apologize again for waking you—" I began.

She waved it off. "We all make mistakes."

"Well, it wasn't precisely a mistake," I said, trying to hold in my irritation. From her viewpoint, she had plenty of reason to be annoyed. "Stacey can show you the video clip of the cold spot and the other readings from the hallway. It's clear something was there, and it moved into your room. Considering the last cold spot turned out to be a pretty scary-looking guy, I was worried for your safety."

"But I was fine." Cherise gave a long yawn. "I'm still so tired."

"I'm not sure you were fine, either." I explained the oily black mass I'd seen floating above her. "If you've been waking up tired, it's probably been feeding on you like that at night."

"I'm waking up tired because my life is nothing but stress," Cherise said.

"I'm sure that's true, too, but what I saw—"

"What *you* saw. What my sister says she saw, which you pretty well just repeated. All I've seen is some blue spots on a thermal camera, and I don't need a detective to tell me this house is drafty and cold."

"Okay." I took a breath. "I hate to pry, but can you tell us what you were dreaming about right before I woke you up?"

Cherise looked at me for a long moment, then

shook her head. "I don't remember."

I didn't think she was telling the truth, but I also didn't think prying onward would get me anywhere. "If you do remember, please let me know. It could give us some critical insight into this entity. And it is the most dangerous entity we've encountered in this house, I believe, because it appears to be feeding on the living. If it's feeding on you, it may be feeding on your little sister, too."

This seemed to trouble her. "How do we know it's dangerous?"

"Only the negative ones prey on the living."

Cherise thought that over a moment, then stood. "I'd better be getting off to Athens. Please stay out of my room. I know I've asked this before, but the request didn't seem to stick."

"All right. Sorry again," I said, feeling chastened and annoyed at the same time. I'd only entered her room because I was worried about her. Cherise wasn't stupid, but she was at least partly in denial.

She left for work, leaving us there as the sun began to rise, and the light through the windows made the house a bit less gloomy. It didn't do much for the chill, though.

There was a queen-sized bed in our borrowed room, and we each had our own sleeping bags. I'm normally very protective of my privacy, but when sleeping at a haunted location, I'd rather have someone else in the room.

I wasn't sure I could sleep here, or even should, given the things I'd observed. The fleabaggish motel was sounding better and better—though a place like that could have plenty of ghosts of its own.

The large antique bed turned out to be absurdly comfortable, though, and soon Stacey was zonked out asleep as if she didn't have a care in the world. Like Cherise, she hadn't seen the ghosts in this house with her own eyes.

I kept thinking over the case while looking at the closed door, expecting something awful to come through. I calmed myself by texting a good morning to Michael, who would be heading to work at the fire station.

It seemed like it would be impossible for me to sleep in that house, but I finally dozed off.

I awoke groggy. I'd been dreaming about my childhood, and I hadn't slept nearly enough sleep, but my phone alarm was beeping me awake. I'd rested until mid-morning, since it would probably not have been a great idea to start cold calling people and asking them strange and random-sounding questions about dead people at five or six in the morning. Ten felt like a more polite hour for such things.

I took my coffee into the front parlor and settled into an old leather chair surrounded by volumes of ancient literature. Stacey was upstairs, reviewing audio and video, an activity that would likely clash with my phone calls.

My first call was to Piper's mother, Annalee. This went direct to voice mail. I identified myself as a private investigator helping with some details of Dr. Marconi's estate, and that I had a few questions about Dr. Marconi that I hoped she could clarify.

My next call, one I dreaded more, was to Marconi's ex-wife, Vera Towning, who'd reverted to her maiden name after the divorce. Her current address was a retirement community near Little Rock, Arkansas.

I decided to stop and have a little more coffee before putting in that call.

As I brewed it in the house's spacious but aging kitchen, my phone rang. Annalee, Piper's mother, calling back already.

"What's this about?" she barked at an ear-bashing volume. She was in her late seventies; maybe she had developed hearing problems.

I identified myself quickly. "I have a couple of quick questions about your late son-in-law, Dr. Marconi, ma'am."

"He passed away."

"Yes, ma'am. Had you been in touch with him recently?"

"What's this about? You said the estate?"

"Yes, ma'am."

"He didn't leave me nothing."

"Oh. Well—"

"Rich old man marries my little daughter and don't even put me in the will. Philip's estate can kiss my buttered grits."

"Well... I'm sorry to hear that, ma'am," I said, not sure how else to respond. "Were you, by any chance, in contact with Dr. Marconi recently? Before his demise?"

"Why do you want to know?"

"We are trying to put together a picture of his

final days. Just ticking some boxes. Can you tell us anything about his state of mind?"

"His state of mind?" She sounded confused at first, then took a little gasp. "Is this about life insurance?"

"Not necessarily."

"Oh, it is, isn't it? I doubt I'm named on that, either. Who is it? That little black girl he left everything to? You working for her?"

I was again taken aback. "Ma'am—"

"I think we all know what was happening there," Annalee chuckled, fairly harshly. "Should have seen it coming. Third time's the charm, I guess. She was the one lucky enough to be with him when he finally croaked out and left it all behind."

"If you're referring to Ms. Edmunds, she's only receiving a small stipend for a temporary period."

"Uh-huh. And the house, from what I hear."

"She's only boarding there while she catalogs his collection."

"So she stays in the mansion and gets a paycheck, while nobody else gets nothing. And she didn't even have to marry him."

I tried to keep focused on the information I needed. "Can you tell us anything about Dr. Marconi's state of mind—"

"I'll tell you what, Miss Represents the Estate, I'll talk for a fee, how about that? Everybody else is getting paid for this, she's getting paid, you're getting paid, why don't I get paid? I gave my daughter, didn't I? And I got nothing."

"A fee?"

"Yes, ma'am."

"Okay. I guess... I could spare twenty or thirty dollars."

She snorted. "You must not want this information too bad."

"What were you thinking?"

"More like... well, a good thousand would be nice."

"A thousand?" I didn't even know how to respond. "I don't have anything—"

"It's the *estate*'s money, ain't it? Everybody else is reaching into this dead man's pocket. I just want a little for myself. I got bills, same as everybody."

"I just don't think it's possible. I wish I could come up with that kind of money, but I have a very limited budget here."

"So do I, honey. So do I." And she hung up on me, taking a tough stance in what was apparently a financial negotiation.

After a short break to shake off those unexpected consequences and eat a quick breakfast, I took a deep breath and called Vera. While I still dreaded this call, it seemed unlikely that it could go much worse than the previous one.

I was able to get Vera on the phone right away— a rarity these days, someone answering a call from an unknown number. I'd expected voice mail. I did my best to steel my nerves before plunging into the cold water of this conversation with the dead man's ex-wife.

Her data-fusion profile had told me that she'd worked for a few public high schools as a performing arts teacher, finally retiring near her last teaching job in Arkansas.

She was stiff and reserved as I gave her the same basic vague story I'd given Annalee.

"I wouldn't know anything about his state of mind," Vera replied. "I hadn't spoken to him in years. He was a distant and distasteful aspect of my past that I have long since put away. Wisdom comes from our mistakes, but they are cruel teachers. He was the cruelest."

"Did you hear about his recent demise?"

"I considered sending flowers, but could not find any quite ugly enough."

I held back a laugh. "From your experiences with him, do you think it was possible he was suicidal? Was he given to depression?"

A long pause. "Would he have killed himself? Let me tell you about Philip. When we met, he was a young star on campus. He'd just landed a book contract, too, though it was quite a while before the book came out. That stupid *Charms and Curses* book was a mild pop-culture ripple in its day, during those foolish years when crystals and Ouija boards were trendy.

"He was my teacher for an undergraduate American history class. Just a standard core requirement. I wasn't even a history student. My major was accounting back then, because my father said I should learn business skills.

"Philip was handsome and eloquent. I was flattered by his attention. He seemed to see more in me than anyone else ever had. When I was in the school play, he encouraged me to change my major to theater. And I did. My parents were furious, but I didn't care. He told me I would be a great actor in New York one day, and I believed him. I wanted to believe him, and everything seemed possible. It was the seventies, I was in my twenties, Athens was a wild party town and I never wanted the party to end. I thought to myself, if I marry Philip, it never will. So I accepted his proposal.

"Of course, once we were married, all was subordinate to his career and his desires. We traveled, and he taught in a few interesting places, but there was little talk of my alleged future in the theater. In time, it dawned on me that I was only to perform for him. He was to be my sole audience for life.

"Then the baby came. I don't know how I was supposed to be the great actor while stuck in that old house in the middle of nowhere, caring for a child while he focused on his work. I would go day after day without seeing anyone except the baby, the housekeeper, and occasionally my husband.

"He grew less interested in me, and in our son Victor, especially after little Vic failed to qualify for the gifted program at school. Vic was never as smart as Philip wanted; by the time Vic was about seven or eight, Philip had written the boy off as a loss, as a kind of unwanted pet, and treated him accordingly. Philip was never physically abusive, but he could not have been emotionally colder to that boy.

"The divorce was shocking, but looking back on it, inevitable. Philip felt Victor and I reflected poorly on him; he berated me for giving him what he called 'an empty-headed dud.' And he moved on to someone else: younger, prettier, more talented, another undergraduate. He wanted to start over. His first family was just a first draft to be thrown away. And in my youth, I'd been foolish enough to sign the prenuptials Philip's father had insisted on. The divorce left me with nothing except custody of a child Philip made no pretense of wanting.

"I began teaching high school theater to support us. I did audition for things occasionally, once Victor grew into a teenager and didn't need me around so much. We all have our little gardens of dead dreams, don't we? And sometimes we still try to water and tend those gardens, long after we should know nothing will ever grow there.

"I heard Philip and his new wife gave lavish parties at the mansion, that he'd even expanded that house for her. Why? It was already too big. And he expanded his book collection until they nicknamed his house The Great Library of Philomath. He held court there with his trophy bride.

"It was a bit sad to hear of *her* death. She was probably young and more or less innocent like I'd been. I wonder if she lived long enough to regret the marriage, like I did. Was there a third one after her? I stopped listening to gossip about him over the years."

"Not that I know of," I said.

"To answer your question, there is no way Philip Marconi killed himself. He thought far too much of himself for that. He thought he was above most of humanity. He thought others should be sacrificed to him, not the other way around."

I'd made several notes. That was one vote against suicide, then—from someone who knew him well but had been out of touch for many years. I'd picked up a lot of background, too.

"I appreciate your help," I said. "During the time you were together, did Marconi spend a lot of time researching the occult?"

"Folklore. I don't think 'occult' is correct."

"Nothing involving communication with the dead?" I was trying to verify whether Marconi's study and practice of necromancy had really started after Piper's death.

"Goodness. I don't think so. Well, we did have a Ouija board party one October. The ghost of Elvis Presley spoke to us. I'm fairly certain our friend was pushing the planchette."

"What was Elvis's message?"

"Don't step on my shoes."

"Sounds like him to me," I said, and the elderly lady chuckled. "Thank you so much for your time."

"My time isn't worth what it once was," she said. "Especially since they took the *Murder, She Wrote* reruns off my TV service."

"I'm sorry to hear that. Jessica Fletcher was an amazing woman."

"I'm auditioning for *Steel Magnolias* at the community theater next week. Perhaps that will fill the afternoons instead."

"Oh, good luck. One last question: during your time at the house, did you ever have any unusual experiences?"

"I can't begin to answer that question."

"Anything that could have been interpreted as paranormal or supernatural," I clarified. I'd saved this question for last since it was the kind that often caused people to hang up. The bridge-burning question.

"Are you asking me if the house was haunted?"

"Only if you had any such experiences there, or if you heard of anyone who did."

"I don't see how this could be of concern to an estate investigation," she said. "But no. There was the family graveyard. I didn't like going back there. Didn't like thinking of myself getting buried there one day. And now I won't be. That's a relief. They can bury me just about anywhere but there."

I thanked her again and ended the call. She'd given me a lot to think about. So had Annalee, despite her general hostility and lack of cooperation. Even that had told me something.

The more I learned about Piper's short life and sudden death, the more I understood why she might be spending her afterlife weeping. Hopefully we could help her move on.

Chapter Fourteen

"I've got something for you," Stacey told me in a singsong voice when I stepped into the room.

"Great. Let's have a look."

"There's not much to see, but there's much to hear." Stacey angled a monitor toward me. "This is from Ye Olde Marconi Family Cemetery, established 1901."

"Piper Overbrook Marconi," my voice said, from when I'd stood at the young woman's grave, and I went on asking questions. "If there's anything you want to say—"

"Help me."

"—you can tell us. We're listening."

"Wait!" I said, talking over my recorded self.

"Did you hear that?"

"I did." Stacey zeroed in on it. The ghost's voice was pretty flat, but sounded female. "I had to isolate it from the wind and the rustling leaves. And slow it way, way down. Yes, I'm amazing, and you're welcome."

"Help me."

On the recording, my voice continued: "How did you feel about your husband?"

"Help me."

"Did you love him? Were you happy with him? Or did you have regrets?"

The wind picked up and tree limbs creaked.

"Are you still here, haunting the house?"

"I don't belong here."

I jumped and pointed. Stacey nodded, grinning wider. "I had to slow that one down, too. It was like a fast little squeak at first."

"Do you feel trapped?" I asked on the recording. "Are you upset that your husband brought you back after your death, Piper?"

A shriek of wind and creaking, groaning limbs sounded from the recording, loud enough to make me wince.

"Sorry." Stacey stopped the recording. "That's it, anyway."

"'Help me,'" I repeated. "'I don't belong here.' She doesn't belong in the cemetery?"

"I mean, she kinda does, though," Stacey said. "She's dead, there's a big headstone with her name on it, and she's buried next to her husband. Where else would she belong?"

I nodded. "It reminds me of what his first wife Vera just told me."

"You talked to Vera?"

"She gave me an earful, thankfully. He encouraged her to be an actress, said they'd go to New York and make it all happen for her. Then they got married and suddenly she's a housewife, pretty much all alone out here in this isolated house while he's out getting on with his life."

"So New York was just a fairy tale. Like Oz. Or Magicia."

"Sure. She felt trapped. Then the professor divorced her."

"And she went to New York?"

"By then she had a son, so it ended up being North Carolina and community theater. And teaching high school drama."

"That's cool. Drama kids need love, too."

"But during her time here, married to him, she felt trapped and increasingly hopeless. I wonder if Piper felt the same. Feels the same, even now."

"So is Piper the big dark cloud thing?" Stacey asked. "Is she feeding on Cherise at night?"

"I'm not sure. If she is, then she's turned into a malevolent entity, some kind of emotional vampire. Gremel seems to be in conflict with the dark cloud. He sent me after it. Did you get any video of him on night vision?"

"I only saw his cold spot on thermal. I still have to go through all that upstairs hallway data. I've been focusing on the cemetery. Maybe we caught an image of Baron von Jerkin."

"Wait til you see this guy. Anyway, that was his only message to me. Pointing at Cherise's room. I think he wanted me to see what was happening to her. And honestly, I don't think I would have stormed in there otherwise. I might have pounded and yelled some more until she woke up, I guess."

"And all of us going in there chased the thing away."

"Yeah. How are you feeling, energy-wise?"

"Great. I'm on my second four-hour energy drink in two hours." Stacey shook an empty aluminum can.

"So, what about when you woke up?"

"Super groggy, but it's hard to sleep in this place."

"Do you remember any dreams?"

"Not really. Oh, yeah. Something about my brother and me playing as kids. He had a water gun or something, and he was laughing as I blasted him with the hose. I was really letting him have it. Wait, why do you want to know?"

"Which brother?"

"Kevin," she said, more quietly. He was her older brother who'd died exploring a haunted house when they were teenagers. I'd suggested to Stacey that we could go back to what remained of that old house, and trap or otherwise eliminate the entity there, but she insisted she wasn't ready.

"I woke up exhausted, too," I told her. "And I dreamed of my father. We were practicing my softball pitch, so I was definitely pretty young. He kept having me throw balls at him. 'Faster, harder,

Ellie!' he'd say. 'More energy!' Maybe that was the entity, literally telling me to feed it my energy."

"So you think the cloud was feeding on us in our sleep?" Stacey asked.

"Possibly. I wonder if it was making Cherise experience happy memories, too," I said. "She wasn't happy about being woken up."

"Happy memories could distract you from the evil thing feeding on you, huh? Like the stuff in mosquito saliva that keeps you from noticing the bite until after the mosquito's gone."

"Interesting thought," I said.

Cherise called me to say Dr. Anderson was traveling but would call us sometime the next day.

I took my phone out into the hall and caught Cherise up quickly. "Marconi's ex-wife is a wealth of information, but Piper's mother Annalee demanded money to talk to us. She feels entitled to some of the estate because of her daughter."

"How much?"

"I offered thirty dollars. She wanted a thousand. We didn't exactly come to terms."

"Do you think she has useful information?"

"She lives hours away, and we don't even know that she was in touch with Marconi. Did he ever mention Annalee or speak to her while you were around?"

"His late wife's mother? I can't say he brought her up, no. Offer her two or three hundred. She'll take that if she's asking a thousand."

"Are you serious?" I was surprised. "That seems like a lot."

"I need this resolved," Cherise said. "I only have ten months left to finish this. My sister and I need to settle into a productive routine right away, and it's not going to happen until something changes around here."

"Okay, but I'm not convinced Annalee has anything to say that's worth that kind of money."

"Don't worry about it. Pay her. I'll cover it."

Her attitude surprised me, given how tight their financial situation was. But maybe that was the point; they really needed that year-end bonus.

"Okay, I'll offer," I said, letting my disappointment sound clear in my tone. "We'll keep plugging away."

"I hope it doesn't take much longer. Do you have a plan for resolving all of this?"

"We have our psychic friend coming out on Saturday night. If Piper is lost between worlds, we can help her move on. The German ghost, the one we think might be Johann Gremel, could simply be attached to the book, in which case we just remove the book from the household. As for the dark cloud... once we identify who or what that is, we can put together a plan for it, too."

"Why not just remove the book now?"

"Because Gremel may be trying to protect us or warn us," I said. "It's the third entity, the dark cloud, that worries me, and it's the one we know the least about. But it seems drawn primarily to you. It could be worth trying to set one of our traps for it in your room. You could stay in another room for the night. If we can trap it, we don't really need to understand it."

"A ghost trap?" Cherise sounded beyond skeptical. "It's time for my class. I'll talk to you later."

I wandered down to the kitchen and grabbed some coffee, extra strong. I would need it before talking to Annalee again. It was hard to believe I'd be offering that lady good money for what was likely useless background information.

Turning my pad to a fresh page, I took a deep breath and called Annalee back.

"I told you there's loose money to be had," is how Annalee answered my call, so I guess she'd saved my number from earlier. I suppose she'd been right about the money, too.

"I've been authorized to offer two hundred dollars for your cooperation," I said.

"And I said I ain't opening up for less than a thousand."

"To be honest, there are doubts about whether you really have anything to offer. We are just trying to tie up loose ends about Dr. Marconi's final days."

"Trying to jack someone out of life insurance, you mean." She chuckled. "If you come back with two hundred, it means you can pay more. Leaving yourself room to wiggle. I know all about it."

"Three hundred was the maximum amount. And I'm not sure it's going to be worth it."

"Didn't nobody understand my daughter and her husband like I did," she said. "Three hundred dollars, I'll tell you whatever you want to know."

"Okay. Let's confirm your mailing address for the check—"

"Oh, honey, I ain't falling for the old check's-in-the-mail routine. I invented that routine."

"Well, you're several hundred miles away."

"You can send it through my Etsy store. I got some crocheted potholders on sale there, too. Cute yarn ones with big old eyes. You might order a couple."

"I might," I said, doubting it.

When the payment had been sent, charged to my Eckhart Investigations credit card, Annalee confirmed it on her end. "Now what all do you want to know, honey?" I guess I was *honey* now that I'd sent her money. Her tone had certainly gone syrupy sweet.

"Everything you know," I said. I started the call-recording app on my phone. "What was your impression of Dr. Philip Marconi? Let's start with when you first met."

"After my daughter went off to college and come back engaged to him," Annalee said. "So that was something, all right. He was a rich man, grew up that way, what you might call a well-bred gentleman, and he knowed a prize filly when he saw one."

"What do you mean? Like a horse?"

"I'm talking about my little Pipette. I trained her up good and pretty, told her how important it was to find the right man—don't repeat Momma's mistakes, I'd say, find you a solid, sturdy man. Aim high. Well, she married a rich man, but I think she could have done better, tell you the truth."

"Did you have doubts about their marriage?"

"He was a few years older. I mean a few years

older than *me*, and he's marrying my daughter. He
should have married me, if anything, but I guess I
weren't what he was looking for at all. If we'd met
when I was my daughter's age, he would have
thought I was something, I'll bet the car on that, but
he just saw me as his girlfriend's country-bumpkin
mother. He looked down on me. Oh, he tried to hide
it, but it poured off him anyhow. Every little look or
word, you could tell he thought I was beneath him."

"Did he treat Piper that way, too?"

"Oh, she measured up, and not just because of
her pretty face. Piper always liked fine things. And I
don't mean like a new motorcycle or a jet ski, but
fancy old books and looking at art and all. Once I
took her to that big art museum in Jacksonville, and
she just wanted to spend all day there, staring away at
one painting or another like they was hypnotizing
her. I don't know what she saw in them paintings to
make her act like that.

"Anyway, that was Pipette, my little fancy pants.
He built that library for her. I guess he had lotsa
books already, but he bought more, even made his
house bigger just to make her happy. They had big
parties with lots of young people. Maybe it was fun
while it lasted, but it didn't last long before my baby's
heart give out. If only we'd knowed how little time
she had left."

"It must have been hard."

"It's still hard. I hoped for grandbabies and all,
but instead I got nothing."

"I understand he also built your daughter a
dance studio in their home. Do you know what plans

she had for the future? Maybe choreography or teaching dance?"

"I don't know anything about a dance studio. I don't see why she'd need to work after marrying him."

"Maybe she just wanted to."

Annalee snorted. "I suppose a person could. I don't know that she had such plans, but it don't matter. She didn't have time for plans. It was all over fast."

"Did you stay in touch with Dr. Marconi after Piper's death?"

"Now and again, I suppose."

"In what context?"

"What's that?"

"When did you speak to him?"

"Well, there was Piper's funeral," she said. "And I called him a couple of times when I was in a pinch and needed a little cash."

"Did he help out?"

"Of course not. I wasn't nearly young and pretty enough to get his wallet open. And he only got colder after Pipette died. After a while he didn't even return my calls."

"Your calls asking for financial help?"

"Exactly. He turned greedy."

"When was the last time you spoke to Dr. Marconi?"

"To him and not his voice mail? Oh, I'd say ten, maybe fifteen years ago."

"So you really can't tell me about his state of mind in his final months. What his mood was like." I was getting annoyed she'd demanded so much money.

"No, but he was only about four years older 'n me, and I can tell you there's plenty to hate about being this age. The worst of it's knowing things will never get better, only worse, until you finally fall apart that last time. Down, down, down, right to the bottom and never up again. That's all there is to think about, especially when you've got nobody and nothing left."

"I'm... sorry," I said, not sure how to respond to that.

"You don't need to say sorry to me. It's gonna happen to you, too."

"Oh. Yeah, possibly." I fought a weird sudden urge to call Michael and push him to get married. I was still in my twenties, and I wasn't sure Michael was the guy I wanted to marry, but she made time seem short and we would all die miserable and alone if we didn't make plans. I shook it off and told myself not to let her get under my skin.

"Let me tell you something about men—" she began.

"I would like to hear more about Piper instead," I said, cutting off whatever long and winding road she was trying to start down. "Why exactly do you think she married him?"

"He had what she wanted. Plenty of money for one, but also all that culture, making her feel like she'd be somebody important."

"Were you in favor of her marrying him?"

"I ain't going to come between my baby girl and

a million dollars. He weren't even that bad looking."
She chuckled.

"So you supported her choice?"

"Well, sure. I wanted her to be able to provide
for her momma in her old age, didn't I? Didn't turn
out that way, though. Now all I can do is hope she
was happy while it lasted."

"How do you think she felt about her marriage?"

"Well, she sounded right happy until she got
sick. Big parties and such. Impressed her little
college friends. If she was sad, it was 'cause she got
sick and died while she was at the top of things. It all
come down real fast for her."

"Did you visit her in the hospital?"

"Course I did. It was hard to see her so little and
pale, her heart dying. She was always so full of
energy, cartwheeling around everywhere. Then she
was gone. Watching your only child go, it's like
watching the future end. Ain't no future after that,
just reruns in your mind."

At this point, I didn't feel so bad about her
grifting the three hundred bucks off us.

"Did you visit their home in Philomath very
often?" I asked.

"I went as much as I got invited, but that weren't
much. I wasn't fit to be seen by their group of
friends, I guess."

"At any time, did you experience anything
unusual there?"

"Like what?"

"Something that could be interpreted as highly
abnormal. Even supernatural."

"Supernatural? You mean was the house haunted?" Annalee sounded surprised by the question. People sometimes do.

"Or did it seem to be that way?" I asked. "Did you ever experience anything along those lines? Or did your daughter ever report anything?"

"Why you asking this?"

"It's a sort of unofficial question about the real estate," I said. "We can't put anything into the official written record, but with these older properties, there are sometimes... well, yes. Hauntings."

"I know it!" she said. "Once I lived with this man who had a house outside Waycross. Late at night you'd sometimes hear pots and pans banging around in the kitchen when there weren't nobody there. Jimmy said it was his mother's ghost trying to fix him some food, and maybe I should try doing the same. I told him you can't cook without groceries, and they ain't free. He was hairy and bristly like a hog, too. I didn't stay around long for that."

"So you see why it's a necessary question," I said. "Did anyone have such experiences in the Philomath house?"

"Not that I heard of. Old place like that probably has its share of ghosts, though. Wouldn't be surprised at all."

"Thank you for all your help. I'll call back if any follow-up questions arise."

"You do that, honey. And look at them potholders again. They make great gifts. I do 'em any color you like."

"I will, thanks."

I hung up and looked over the pad of notes I'd collected. Maybe the place did have some old ghosts, but so far nobody had reported trouble with any before Aria and Cherise moved in. It looked like the real problems had indeed begun with Dr. Marconi's occult experiments, not before.

Chapter Fifteen

"We have unidentified dark cloud and one recently deceased former owner from whom we've heard nothing," I said, pacing in the spare bedroom while Stacey watched me, the videos on her monitors paused.

"Yeah, where is that guy?" Stacey asked.

"It's possible Dr. Marconi moved on peacefully after his death, leaving behind his library of occult texts and artifacts, the ghosts he summoned, and the old family home that he'd rebuilt and expanded to reflect his personality and impress his wife... but it doesn't feel right, does it? A guy like that dies suddenly in his home, possibly by accident, possibly pushed by a ghost—and no part of him lingers around in this haunted environment he created? Like I said, it's possible, but really hard to buy."

"Like the oat-and-craisin Stoneground bars," Stacey said, nodding. "They're always out of stock. So you're saying maybe the dark cloud is Marconi?"

"It seems to fit. The guy gets deep into the occult during life, maybe he becomes a dangerous ghost soon after death, because it's like he's in a familiar world."

"His own brier patch."

"Right. And if it's him, he's already feeding on the living. Turning into a parasite. He could very likely morph into a demonic entity over time. That process usually takes centuries. Most ghosts move on in that time, as their ties to the living world crumble. The ones who don't tend to be the very worst."

"So he could morph faster?"

"Yes. Because he's doing it deliberately. He's not blindly groping his way into a method of occasionally feeding on the living, a hungry ghost desperate for energy. He probably knows feeding on the living will make him more powerful, and he's doing it as much as he can."

"While distracting us with happy dreams."

"Except for Aria," I said.

"Yeah, why not her?" Stacey asked. "Why didn't it feed on her?"

I shook my head. "I'm not sure. Usually the kid in the house is a negative entity's prime victim— more energy to feed on, more naivety to exploit. Maybe the other spirits are protecting her somehow."

"Maybe she reminds Piper of herself," Stacey

said. "You know, young and vulnerable, stuck in this house."

"But Cherise should remind Piper of herself even more. A college student brought out here by Marconi, now living here and feeling isolated."

"So maybe Baron von Jerkin's been protecting Aria?"

I nodded. "When the sound of crying drew Aria out of her room, toward the dark doors, it was Gremel who scared Aria back to her room. It happened consistently enough that she thought they were two sides of the same entity."

"Ooh, like the library ghost in *Ghostbusters*. One minute she's just quietly looking at books and shushing people, the next she's a screaming monster. Then the opening credits start."

"But here there are two different entities. Aria follows the sound of the weeping girl to the dark doors, and Gremel charges out to scare Aria back. So what might have happened without Gremel?"

"She would've had some kind of encounter with Piper's ghost. Huh. Why's Gremel worried about Piper? You think maybe Piper's been the dark cloud all along?" Now Stacey stood and paced like me, which really crowded up the spare bedroom's primary pacing zone. I couldn't tell if she was doing it to make fun of me or not. "Maybe there's no ghost of Dr. Marconi, because he totally moved on. But Piper, after being dragged back from the other side, dragged into haunting this house against her will... maybe *she* evolved over time. But what's with the weeping, if she's the powerful and dominant ghost here?"

"The weeping might have been a useful weapon against Marconi," I said. "Opening him up emotionally, enabling her to feed on him. In his journal, he describes her always seeming unhappy. She would lie beside him in bed like a freezing cold cloud—"

"And we saw a cloud over Cherise's bed!" Stacey said. "So... Piper's learned to feed on the living, and she's trying to apply the methods that worked for her with Marconi. That's why she's weeping. It's an emotional trap. Wow, we've got it all figured out! Maybe."

"It's a hypothesis," I said. "It fits what we have so far. But she's taking a different approach with Aria—drawing her out of the room, down the hall. Like she has special plans for Aria."

"You mean possession?"

"It's possible. Maybe Piper's ghost is stronger inside the master suite and it wants to lure her in there. Late at night. Alone. The whole incurable-sadness approach worked for her before, with Marconi, so she goes with what she knows. She lets Aria hear her cry and hopes it draws her close. Draws her sympathy and her curiosity."

"Crying probably works better for that," Stacey said. "I mean, if the ghost was screaming, or moaning, or knocking things around, that wouldn't draw anyone close."

"It would put her guard up. While crying could elicit sympathy instead. Especially from someone young and innocent."

"Exactly!" Stacey said, and we nearly collided in our pacing, so I sat down.

"So we could be down to two active entities instead of three," I said. "And we should consider baiting the ghost trap for Piper as well as Philip."

"Let's rummage around in their room for personal things." Stacey started for the door.

Down the hall, we found the dark doors locked again.

"Do they lock automatically when you close them?" Stacey wondered, tugging on a doorknob.

"The doors at the other end don't. Let's go around. I don't want to risk damaging anything with lock picks if I don't have to."

We went down the long front stairs and through the first-floor hall, past the now-familiar reading room and study with its massive desk and antique bar, everything upholstered in leather or paneled in wood; it was a few deer heads and a cloud of tobacco smoke short of being an old-time men's club out of the nineteenth century.

The library was dim, with its lights off and many of its windows shuttered. I looked toward the Tomb Room concealed behind its bookshelf-lined door.

We clambered up the steep stairs toward a second-story walkway, up into the late professor's hanging garden of books.

"Is it just me, or does this feel more rickety than last time?" Stacey whispered.

"I think it's creaking and shaking more," I said, and I wasn't kidding. It felt less stable to me.

I paused to look up at the spot above us with the

broken railing where the professor had fallen, where we'd seen the girl in the window. We'd focused some observation gear there the previous night, but hadn't gone through the data collected yet. There were still countless hours of video and audio from all over the house to pore through.

The walkway did seem creakier than before as we approached the dark doors, the rear entrance to the master suite, and heaved them open.

No sunlight penetrated the dim hallway and rooms beyond, any more than over in the Tomb Room. The closed shutters kept the suite dark and claustrophobic-feeling; the rooms here were spacious but somehow felt small, as if the walls and ceiling were pressing in, as if the placed wanted to push us out, or maybe to crush us. The air was stifling and stale, hard to breathe.

We searched for personal items in the master bedroom, which seemed about as personal an area as we could search. We found their wedding rings, recognizable from their portraits. Piper's was in a small chest of pricey jewels. She seemed to favor gold and sapphires, as if to match her hair and eyes. Her wedding ring had an impressive boulder of a diamond.

Dr. Marconi's ring was an easier find, sitting on the dark end table by the bed, golden like hers but with smaller diamonds.

"Man, her ring alone must be worth thousands of dollars," Stacey said. "Should we use something cheaper?"

"We're looking for maximum sentimental value

here," I told her. "If the black cloud is Piper, she might be drawn to it. If it's Philip, well, he's obsessed with her, so same thing."

"Unless she was unhappy in her marriage and the ring just reminds her of bad times."

"Either way, surely she's connected emotionally to it, and might be drawn close enough to check it out."

We hauled in the big stamper that seals the ghost traps at high speed, taking it in large pieces up the long staircase and assembling it in Cherise's room. We set a ghost trap inside—a cylindrical leaded-glass jar surrounded by electrified wire mesh insulated by clear plastic. The basic design dates back more than a century, but the insulating plastic layer was wisely added somewhere in the twentieth century. We mounted the trap's lid a couple feet above, ready for the stamper to slam it down.

"Are we turning it on?" Stacey asked as I tested the sensors. A spike in electromagnetic energy combined with a drop in temperature would trigger the trap to slam shut.

"We'll wait until tonight."

Stacey and I napped that afternoon to get refreshed for the night's observation. We didn't want to wake up drained, facing a ghost that was all amped up after feeding on our energy, so we avoided sleeping in the house.

Despite the chill, we slept in Stacey's pretty nice and roomy tent in a relatively clear patch of the weedy, thorny back yard. I had to agree that our sleeping bags were more comfortable than the drop-down cots in the van, and the tent was much less spooky than being inside the house. Stacey was a little too enthusiastic about turning this into a camping trip. At least the mosquitoes weren't out yet.

The alarm woke us at sunset. It was time to go to work.

Chapter Sixteen

"I still think y'all are crazy," Cherise said, sitting in one of the chairs in the spare bedroom that Stacey and I had been borrowing. She looked over the monitors and laptops set up on the dresser and in the empty wardrobe, showing locations around the house. One now focused on the ghost trap in Cherise's room. "And that contraption is even crazier than the idea that ghosts are walking the house at night."

"If nothing else, maybe we'll find some solid evidence for you out of this," I said.

"Are you still saying you think *nothing* weird is going on in this house?" Aria asked her sister. Aria was pacing the middle of the room, just as I'd done earlier.

"I'm coming around," Cherise said, averting her eyes like the topic made her uncomfortable.

"Well, we totally appreciate you letting us try, even though it seems wacky," Stacey said. "I've seen these ghost traps work before. It's all a matter of dropping the right lure in the right spot. Just like fishing."

"I've never gone fishing," Cherise said.

"Oh, you should try it!" Stacey told her.

"Okay," I said, cutting in before Stacey could start planning a fishing trip for all of us. No thanks. "I'm getting into position."

"Are y'all sure I should stay here?" Aria said. She wore her headphones, but her tablet was darkened for the moment. "Won't the ghosts suspect something if I'm not in my own room like usual?"

"If this goes wrong, we could provoke the entity into an unpleasant response," I said. "I'd rather everyone be together."

"But you'll be alone," Aria argued.

"Aria, enough," Cherise said.

"I won't, because you'll all be watching over me," I said.

"Uh, okay." Aria didn't look impressed.

"Good luck," Cherise told me before I walked out of the room. She was wearing my leather jacket as part of a fairly weak bid to confuse the ghosts about who was who.

"Thanks." I closed the door and walked up the hall to her room. I wore Cherise's extra-long flannel pajama shirt over my own shirt and jeans. I doubted our clothing swap would really fool any spirits for long, but it couldn't hurt.

I turned off the hallway light, leaving the house dark and quiet before I stepped into Cherise's room.

I closed the door and switched off the light. It was time to bait the trap.

The two wedding rings clinked against the leaded glass as I dropped them to the bottom of the trap. Then I lit the slow-burning candles inside.

While most ghosts are averse to too much light, like sunlight or pure white light, they also need to draw energy from their environment if they're going to do anything. This creates cold spots.

Some will feed on the raw bit of fire offered by a candle flame. Long before thermal cameras and EMF meters, my predecessors in the ghost-hunting trade would use candles as ghost sensors, watching for the candles to flicker, dim, or snuff out.

With the trap set, I gave a thumbs up to the night vision camera, then climbed into Cherise's bed and pulled the quilted comforter up to my head, concealing most of my face.

I lay in the dark, letting my eyes adjust to the low, flickering candlelight. The stamper looked out of place among the antique furniture, like some weird spindly robot.

The unfamiliar room soon filed with shadowy, potentially threatening shapes, the way strange dim rooms tend to do. Though pitch blackness is often worse, serving as a blank canvas for the frightened imagination; plus, you won't see anything creeping up close until it grabs you.

My mind was ready to play tricks on me, to tell me that a dark shape occupied the antique chair I could barely see in the corner, and someone tall and slender watched me from the partially ajar closet door. Why hadn't I closed that?

I looked to the cameras pointed at me. The night vision would be showing me in weird shades of green, the thermal probably showing my body in red, oranges, and yellows. It felt weirdly invasive to know they were watching, but of course I was glad Stacey was there if I needed backup.

Time passed. The house grew silent, aside from occasional creaking and groaning. The wind rattled limbs outside whenever it picked up, and it sounded like creatures climbing the outside of the house.

Down the hall, the lights would be out, the three of them sitting in darkness, watching the glow of the screen. We were pretending the entire household had gone down to sleep for the night.

More time passed, slowly. I was alone with my thoughts. I would rather have been alone with some ice cream. I really should have planned my week better.

The house creaked, the shadows shifted in the candlelight like dark figures watching me from around the room. I waited and watched, doing my best pretense of being asleep.

It was hours before it happened.

"Cold spot," Stacey whispered over headset, her voice crackling with interference though she was just down the hall. "Sliding your way like a penguin down a snowboard slope."

I tapped the headset's microphone gently to acknowledge I'd heard.

"It's coming in there with you," Stacey whispered, even lower. "Be careful, Ellie."

I kept my narrowed, barely-cracked eyes on the door. I really should have closed them completely, but I just couldn't bring myself to do it.

The room grew noticeably colder. The floor creaked not far away—it could have been a footstep.

I shivered, watching, forcing myself to remain still and act asleep.

All the little hairs on my arms rose, as if an electrical storm were gathering right around me. I couldn't see anything, but I could feel something in the room with me, the way you know when someone is watching you from behind even when you can't see them.

The candle mounted highest inside the trap fluttered, and I caught my breath. If the entity entered the trap and we caught it, then determining its identity and motives wouldn't matter so much. We could physically remove it from the house and bury it far away.

The only question would be where to release it. One option was a distant but pleasant old cemetery, like the one full of wildflowers and trees in the ghost town of Goodwell, where an entity could wander openly within the cemetery walls until it finally moved on. The other was to bury the trap, with the entity still inside, in the cursed earth of a certain remote, long-abandoned mountain churchyard ruled by particularly hostile spirits.

For that, it would be nice to know whether the ghost had truly harmed anyone. If it had murdered Dr. Marconi, for example, pushing him through the rickety library railing.

Maybe the railing hadn't truly been all that rickety, I thought. Maybe the ghost was just very strong.

The candle ceased flickering and resumed its solid, steady burn.

"Ellie, it's coming near you," Stacey whispered.

I said nothing, but shivered as the entity moved closer. I couldn't see it, but after a moment, the candlelight from the trap dimmed a bit—not like the candles were burning lower and going out, but more like some kind of filter had moved into place in front of the trap, like a screen door blurring the view.

I tensed, wondering whether I would see anything at all, whether the dark oily cloud would form above me and try to feed. Sometimes these nighttime creepers will take your blanket and slide it off your bed before they come down on you, but nobody in this house had reported anything like that.

Under the blanket, my fingers rested against my flashlight. If the entity attacked, I would blast it, naturally. I was extremely disappointed that it had skirted the trap and kept coming at me instead.

The room grew colder.

"Ellie?" a familiar voice asked. I gasped a little; partly because it hadn't come from my headset. It seemed to originate on the far side of the bed, deeper in the room, near a bookshelf full of dusty leather volumes. I also gasped because of whose voice it was.

I turned my head.

There he was, the candles casting more shadows than light on him, but I knew him. He wore one of his favorite worn checkered shirts over his broad chest, his mustache like some time traveling species of facial hair from the 1970s, as I'd told him when he'd grown it.

"Dad?" I whispered.

He was looking at me with his dark brown eyes, frowning under the awful yet unkillable mustache. I felt disappointment and disapproval radiating from him.

"You shouldn't be here, pumpkin," he said, a nickname he'd only used during a few of my elementary school years. "This house isn't safe. It's full of bad things. And doorways to terrible places."

"But you're free," I whispered. "I saw. You and Mom."

"I only came to warn you. I can't stay long. You have to leave this place."

"I have to protect these people."

"No." He smiled, in the same way he'd done when trying to explain some math homework I'd been struggling with. "You don't have to protect anyone but yourself. Get out tonight, and don't come back."

"What about the people who live here?"

"Their fates are sealed. You cannot help them."

"What?"

"Ellie, I'm not telling you again. Go!" He was

angry and pointing toward the door.

"That's what you're here to say? You traveled all the way here from the other side to tell me to save myself and not help them?"

"Yes." He smiled, looking happy again. "I can't protect you from what's happening here."

"What is happening here?"

"Ellie, it's not for you to know."

I stared at the apparition of my father a long moment. "Stacey, please come here."

"You got it!" she replied, and her running footsteps echoed in the hall outside a moment later.

"What are you doing?" my father asked.

"Just getting a second opinion."

The door opened. Stacey brought no added light to the room, either by flicking the overheads or drawing her flashlight, which was good.

"Ellie?" she asked.

"What do you see?" I pointed.

Stacey drew in a sharp breath. "It's that oily cloud thing. You want me to light it up?"

"No." I stared at the apparition. "You're not my father. Show me your true face."

"Pumpkin, you're confused," he said, but the voice shifted as he spoke, becoming something higher and scratchier than my father's. His face became distorted, the eyes reflective and black like oil. "You listen to your father, or he'll punish you, little pumpkin."

"Tell me your name," I said. "Your true name."

It cackled. My father's face filled with black veins, then ruptured.

"Is it Philip Marconi? Piper Overbrook Marconi? You don't have to stay trapped here. Whoever you are, we can help you move on. You could be free."

"I am free," the increasingly liquid and featureless apparition said. Its voice wasn't especially loud, but it had turned so high pitched and screechy that it felt like fingernails scraping my eardrums. It cackled, the sound of a thing that had not been human in a long time, if ever.

I felt even colder on the inside than on the outside as I realized the entity was perhaps neither Philip nor Piper Marconi, but something much older than either of them.

"Give me your name!" I shouted.

It replied with another ear-scraping cackle. Too smart for the direct approach. Too bad, because its identity would have been news we could use.

As it cackled, unnaturally bright lights filled the windows. A wailing voice boomed like thunder all around us.

Then a loud crash shook the house, as though an earthquake was rattling its foundations. Dust rained from the ceiling. The bed where I sat rattled and shook beneath me. The floor groaned like it would give away and I'd fall right through, and then the shaking roof would come crashing down on top of me.

Chapter Seventeen

The quaking and shaking of the house didn't intensify to kill us all, fortunately, but the strange lights and booming, caterwauling voice continued to blare through the windows.

I jumped to my feet, expecting the shapeshifting dark cloud entity to leap on me, but it had melted out of sight.

In the hall, the noise was louder and the light was brighter. It all came from the front of the house. The glass doors to the balcony glowed as if they'd become an otherworldly portal like Carol Anne's closet in *Poltergeist*.

The voice and music, however, was decidedly this-worldly.

I scrunched up my eyes as though it would help me make out the words. "Is that...?"

"Yep. David Allan Coe," Stacey said, as we reached the door to the spare room.

Cherise and Aria stumbled into the hall to join us, looking toward the light and noise.

"Country music. This house keeps getting worse," Aria muttered.

"What's happening?" Cherise asked, covering her eyes.

"Somebody with high beams and a very effective speaker system is visiting you in the middle of the night," Stacey said.

"Any idea who that could be?" I asked. Cherise shook her head, but not too emphatically.

I walked along the front hall, warily eyeing the balustrade to my left and the long drop to the front stairs beyond it.

The light-filled balcony doors weren't locked. I turned both handles, pushed them open, and stepped outside.

I headed toward the front corner of the balcony to look over the railing at the source of the blinding light and roaring music. The balcony floor felt a bit too spongy and wobbly for my taste.

Below, a large pickup truck had driven up the wide front steps and smashed into one of the front columns supporting the balcony where I stood. Its high beams were on, its driver-side door was wide open, and David Allen Coe sang about how his long hair couldn't cover up his red neck.

Another crash, somewhere below and out of my

line of sight, like breaking glass. One of the windows? Had Cherise locked the front doors? I certainly hoped so.

"What in the name of all that's up is happening out here?" Stacey stood at the balcony doors behind me.

"Someone drove a truck into that column. In a related story, this balcony might be collapsing, so let's step back inside."

In the hall, Cherise and Aria looked understandably panicked. They stared down over the balustrade at the front doors, and they jumped when another smash sounded from that direction.

"Are the front doors locked?" I asked.

"They're all locked," Cherise said. "I don't want random weirdos wandering in at night."

"And you don't have any idea who this random weirdo is?" I looked from her to Aria. "Nobody dated a David Allen Coe fan with a pickup lately, did they?"

"Oh, I know you're not looking at me," Aria said. She asked Cherise, "What about you? Is this a crazed-out friend of yours from school or what?"

Cherise looked uncomfortable but didn't answer.

I walked to the front bedroom where we'd set up our gear and peered out the window. It offered a more complete view of the action: the pickup with its front end wrecked against the column, left there now to idle and to blare light and sound.

The assailant was visible now, a swaying man, unshaven and wild-eyed, who looked like he hadn't seen the inside of a barber shop in a year, or the inside of a laundry room or clothing store in about ten.

He had a case of bottled beer by his feet, and he hurled a bottle against the front wall of the house, where it smashed by the front doors.

"Get out!" he shouted, as I eased up the window pane so I could hear him. This meant we also heard more about David Allan Coe's troubles with being a longhaired redneck. "Get out!"

"That's what everyone keeps saying," I muttered as the others caught up with me and looked out the window. "This guy, Gremel, and my father. 'Get out.'"

"Your father?" Cherise asked.

"Well, the Mr. Oily-Cloud imitation," I said. "The same one who kept telling me to throw the softball harder and faster in my dream. 'More speed, more energy,' he kept saying. 'Give me more energy.' And then I woke up drained."

"Get out of my house!" the man's slurred voice shouted. He drew back another bottle to throw, then seemed to reconsider and drank from it instead.

"I have a guess," Cherise said. "This guy could be Dr. Marconi's son."

"The son has a police record," I said. "Fraud. Drugs. And, I'm going to go way out on a limb and guess he might have something of a drinking problem. We should call the police."

"Wait," Cherise said. "I understand why he's mad."

"Who cares? He can sleep it off in the drunk tank. That's the safest thing for everyone," I told her.

"Hello?" Cherise called through the open window. "Who's there?"

The swaying man belched and looked up at her. His jeans sagged unpleasantly low on his hips, revealing badly worn underpants that I won't describe.

"Who's there?" he shouted back. "Asking me who's there. Like I don't belong here. You don't belong here, that's who don't belong here, if anyone don't... if anyone... don't you... what were you...what?"

"You're Victor, aren't you?" Cherise shouted.

"Vic. Everyone calls me Vic. This is my house. My family. All the way back..." He described a swooping arc with his arm, sloshing his open beer everywhere, and the move threw him off balance. His pants dropped to his knees, and he tumbled backward off the portico and landed in the winter-bare rose bushes, atop countless cold hard thorns. He let out a grunt of pain that we could hear all the way up to the window, even as Coe began to sing about the ghost of Hank Williams driving his otherworldly Cadillac.

"We should go help him," Cherise said. "Aria, you wait here."

"Drunks are dangerous," I countered, but she was already starting for the stairs.

Sighing, I followed after, wondering what made her so concerned for the lunatic who'd just driven his truck up onto the front porch like some crazy character from a David Allan Coe song.

Stacey and I drew our flashlights, ready to use

the beveled forward edge. Designed for SWAT and military use, the tactical flashlights were capable of bashing in windows and the occasional face as needed. I hoped it wouldn't come to that.

I glanced back at Aria, who watched over the balustrade.

"I know," Aria said. "Wait here. That way the ghosts can sneak up behind me and kill me while you're all distracted with Jimmy Smokes Crack out there."

"He's more likely smoking meth. You be ready to call 911 if we need it," I said.

Aria nodded and held up her phone.

We headed downstairs. Cherise swerved into the parlor and opened the window there, not quite willing to give up the protection of the locked doors just yet. I had to approve.

"Vic?" Cherise asked.

A groan sounded from outside. "I got stuck," he said, his tone whiny and miserable.

"Stuck how?"

"Stuck right in my dang... stuck all over. I can't get up. Help me. Please."

"Weren't you just yelling and throwing bottles at the house?" I asked. "How are you making demands now?"

There was a long pause before he answered, and when he did, his voice cracked like one of his beer bottles. "I'm sorry. I'm so sorry. You got to understand."

"I get the feeling he's been through his share of angry break-ups followed by weepy, drunken pleading for forgiveness," Stacey said.

Outside, he struggled and kicked in the rose bushes, lying almost upside down in them, not making much progress in escaping.

He moaned again. "Why, Dad? Why?"

I had to admit, he was going from scary to pathetic fast. The dropping-pants-and-falling-off-the-porch gag had really diminished him.

Cherise sighed and went to the front door.

I led the way out, my flashlight ready in case it turned into a fight.

"Watch out for broken glass," I reminded everyone. Shattered bottles littered the portico, filling the air with the yeasty smell of beer.

The truck was still idling against the column, its front tires parked on the wide stairs.

Beyond that, past the broken bottles and the edge of the porch, Vic lay moaning, tangled in the thorny bushes, or at least too intoxicated to pull free of them and stand up. He was like one of those knights and princes who'd totally failed to reach Sleeping Beauty through the enchanted hedges.

"What are you doing here, Victor?" I asked.

"It's my house," he said, voice slurred, eyes looking up at the stars above. "It's not... fair. My grandfather was born here. My great-grandfather... I think. This was *my* house. The only good part of my life was here. Now he left it all to...to *you*." He turned and glared at Cherise. "Why you?"

"You're confused," I said. "Cherise doesn't own the house. She's only staying here while she catalogs your father's collection."

"Is that what she told you?" He closed his eyes and chuckled.

"Yes. She just works here temporarily."

"Just the help," Victor said, gesturing aimlessly with one hand. "Don't ask me, I'm just the help. No, no. He picked her. He wrecked all our lives for the girl behind door number two. Then she died. Now he left it all to girl number three." He opened one eye and squinted it at Cherise. "I get it. You're cute. Brainy. His type. But he was so old, and you're like a kid. Didn't it make you feel sick, doing that with him?"

"Whatever you might be implying, I never *did* anything with Dr. Marconi!" Cherise snapped. "He could barely get around with a cane. Not even a cool Bond-villain cane, I mean he had one of those kind with four rubber feet."

"So he was old and easy to push around," Vic said.

"I did not push him around, either."

"Then why you? I suffered from him my whole life and got forgotten. So why you?"

"I don't know," Cherise said, quietly, looking at the ground.

"He didn't leave her everything," I tried to explain again. "It's just a temporary job, organizing his things."

"He sort of did," Cherise said, even more quietly.

"What?" I turned to her, confused.

"That's the bonus. If I get the books organized and cataloged in twelve months, the house is mine.

And all the land, which is a couple hundred acres. I become the owner."

"The library, too?" I asked.

"It's my test, to make sure I'm up to it."

"But do you really want to be stuck here?" Stacey asked.

"I don't know about that," Cherise said. "But there's some other things that come with it, too. Real estate."

"Old strip malls and rundown apartment buildings," Vic said. "Mostly in Augusta."

"So his business interests, too?" I asked.

"All my family's stuff, she gets," Vic said. "I get nothing. I can't even get out of this bush. Can anyone help?"

"Wait." I walked over to the truck, killed the engine and stereo, turned off the headlights, and pocketed the keys. Then I walked down the stairs to the ground.

"If we help you out," I said, "No attacking, no beer bottles. You do literally everything we say, or it's right back in the rose bush you go."

"Yeah," he said. "Yeah, I guess that that's fair."

The three of us hauled him out, which involved raking him across many more thorns, but given how he'd made his entrance, I wasn't too concerned for his well-being.

We finally got him down to weedy dirt, where he lay, scratched all over, his pants unfortunately still down around his knees, his ratty boxers badly frayed. Those droopy tangled pants would keep him from getting anywhere too fast, so despite the unpleasant visuals I didn't really want to help him with that situation.

"So you're here for what, exactly?" I looked at his truck. Tennessee plates. "Did you drive all this way tonight?"

"I heard you talked to Mom," he said. "A bunch of questions about Dad. She said you might call me."

"We might have," I said.

"I got a right to know what happens to my family's home," he said. "I got a right to... at least... be part of this for a while. Have one last look. Take a couple things. Nothing important. Just things that matter to me."

"Well, that's something better discussed during business hours, by email, and while sober," I said. "Not by driving into the front of the house and throwing beer bottles at it. So here's what we'll do —"

Whatever I was going to say didn't matter, because flashing blue lights approached from around the next crook in the road. Two police cars.

They flew right up to the house and parked in the driveway.

"Who called the police?" I asked.

"I did. Duh." Aria stood in the doorway, looking out with approval at the approaching police. "Like I was going to just wait around and see if Jimmy Smokes Meth turned out to be a good guy."

"Good would be kind of a stretch," Stacey said, looking at the destruction he'd caused. "Pathetic, maybe."

The county police approached us, and we knew we still had a long night ahead.

Chapter Eighteen

There were complications. Local police had trouble understanding how the man named Marconi, the late professor's son, was not the owner of the house. The house had belonged to their family for more than a century, closer to a century and a half, and the local sheriff knew this quite well.

Still, there was little doubt Vic was drunk and had driven his truck into the house, which would tend to get a man arrested even on his own property.

So the police hauled him away and a wrecker hauled off the truck to the impound.

By the time it was all over, it was nearly sunrise. Aria went off to her room as the early-morning light brightened the sky.

"At least I don't have class on Saturdays,"
Cherise said. "I'm exhausted but too jittery to sleep.
So it's coffee and back to work in the library for
me."

I nodded. "I'll be around, too. I can't say the tent
in the yard feels like the safest spot after all that." I
looked at Cherise a moment. "So it's true? You
inherit everything if you do the job?"

"Yes. I don't understand why Dr. Marconi would
give me so much. At first I didn't know he had a son,
so I thought maybe he just had no one else. Then I
heard..." Cherise shrugged. "Is it strange I feel a little
guilty?"

"No. It's strange that he left you everything, but
his conditions are even stranger. Why do you have to
organize and catalog the library in twelve months if
you're going to own it yourself anyway? On day
three hundred and sixty-six, you could heap up all
the books and burn them if you wanted to. So
what's the rush?"

"The lawyer said it was meant as a test," Cherise
said. "To make sure I'm worthy of the inheritance.
Marconi's words."

"Well, considering his son would probably blow
it all on meth and beer and David Allan Coe records,
I kind of see where he was coming from," Stacey
said.

"What happens to the estate if you don't finish
in time?" I asked.

"It gets broken up and donated to a list of
academic foundations."

"And you're sure there's no reason why this man

you met less than a year ago would leave you everything?"

"Like I said, I don't know! If you're accusing me of sleeping with him, like Victor did, the answer is still 'no.' And also 'gross' because he was in no condition. He could barely hobble around. He was shriveled and hunched. He probably shouldn't have been living alone. He could have—well, he did have an accident."

"Before he died, did he tell you about his intentions with his estate?" I asked.

"Oh, no, I always thought he was about to fire me because he was so cranky."

"This doesn't make sense," I said.

"Yeah. That's what I've been thinking the whole time," Cherise said. "But I figured he was some crazy, lonely old guy, and what could I do? Turn down an estate that could provide for me and my sister for the rest of our lives? And all I had to do was organize a library? How could I say no?"

"You couldn't," I said, mulling that over. "It was basically an offer you couldn't refuse."

Cherise smiled a little. "It was. And that's why I have to get back to work." She headed inside, and Stacey and I followed, closing the front doors against the last chill of the dying winter.

While Cherise headed for the library, Stacey and I went upstairs to regroup. Piles of work awaited us in the form of research, video, audio, and other heaped-up data that needed to be sifted.

"Make sure Jacob's still coming tonight," I told Stacey as I dropped into a chair, feeling both exhausted and keyed up. "I need a medium's perspective on this place. We're back at square one with the dark cloud. We can keep baiting it with Piper and Dr. Marconi's rings, but it didn't really respond to that. After seeing it up close, I think the dark cloud might be something older, maybe something conjured up by Marconi's experiments in necromancy. Either that, or Marconi managed to corrupt and twist himself so hard in life that his soul was already nearly demonic the moment he died."

"Well, the weird ritual room seems like the place to make that happen," Stacey said. "He spent years and years doing who knows what occult craziness in there."

I nodded. "I'm supposed to talk with Dr. Anderson later this morning. I can't exactly grill him because he's Cherise's superior at the history department, but I want to know about his last conversations with Marconi."

"All righty, I texted Jacob. Though if he was a *real* psychic, he would have texted me first."

We got to work. Stacey mostly analyzed footage and checked for anomalies in the collected data. I mostly looked through Marconi's journal and various property records and newspaper stories printed out at the courthouse and library.

Marconi's journal focused entirely on his necromantic romance with his dead wife, giving little insight into what else he might have been up to. Those missing pages were killing me.

"There's so much here," Stacey said, coming up for air from her analysis. She drank green tea while she worked. "I've picked up all kinds of small orbs and drifting cold spots from the library area we're monitoring. I can't say for sure whether they were Piper or Philip or, I guess, 'other.' But you need to see your run-in with Baron von Jerkin and the dark cloud." She brought up the thermal clip, the red and yellow curves of my body, which always felt a little weird to look at, and the cold blue blob of Gremel, the icy core of him not much larger than a baseball, hovering in front of me.

"Is there another spirit in there?" my recorded voice asked. Was my voice really that annoying? I came off brusque and pushy, I thought, nothing like Stacey's softer Alabama accent that made everything sound like an invitation to cake and tea. "Is it Piper? Or someone else?"

"Hear that?" Stacey asked, pausing it.

"No."

"Neither did I, the first time I watched this. But let me amplify it a bit... "

She did, and now I heard it: a throaty growling sound, almost like a wolf.

"More German?" I asked.

"I think so."

The voice remained throaty and deep, but at the enhanced volume, it was clearly saying a word or two.

"Play it again," I said, and she did. I listened carefully to make sure I'd heard it right, but it made no sense to me. "Off-hocker?"

"Maybe it's got a sore tooth and thinks it's talking to a cop," Stacey said. "I schwear, off-hocker,

I just went to da dennist."

"I'm sure it's German," I began, but then my phone rang. It was time for my chat with Dr. Anderson, who looked like my last chance to shake out any details about the late professor from those who'd known him in life. I almost always go to see witnesses in person, but for this case, two witnesses were hundreds of miles away, in different directions. Anderson was much closer, but I had to handle him gently and quickly to avoid any risk of getting Cherise in trouble at work.

"I have to take this," I told Stacey while I stepped out into the hall. The pacing area was better out there.

I answered and found myself talking to the professor's assistant, who then brought the professor on the line, since he was clearly way too important to wait those extra couple of seconds while the phone rang on my end.

"Leonid Anderson," he said, by way of greeting.

I introduced myself quickly. "I really appreciate you taking the time to speak with me."

"I'm afraid I don't have much time to spare, but I wanted to get this in before the weekend. I'm unclear exactly what this is about."

"I'm a private investigator working with Dr. Marconi's estate," I said, vaguely, then steamrolled ahead before he could ask for details. "And we only have a couple of questions. First, were you in contact with the professor in the days before he died?"

"I wouldn't say we were in contact. I hadn't

heard from him in years before he reached out and said he needed a qualified researcher to straighten out his collection."

"What kind of qualifications was he looking for?"

"Someone with a dexterity for languages, for one. Romance, Germanic, ancient Greek, Latin, both ancient and medieval Church, ideally. We didn't have anyone floating around who met *all* of his criteria, but Cherise was extremely well-rounded. Moreover, she had the rigorous self-discipline and the economic need that he was looking for."

"Economic need?"

"Well, yes. I am sure his concern was partly humanitarian, but he also wanted, as he put it, someone hungry and hardworking. But someone deserving as well."

"What else did he say about what he wanted?" I tried to keep my tone light and casual, even bored, like I was reading from a list, but it was actually critical for me to get every detail here.

"Well, obviously someone highly intelligent and organized. Someone with a love of history, but that's all of us around here." He chuckled a little.

"Is that all?"

"Generally, yes."

"Are you sure there's nothing else?"

"I may have to check my notes and get back to you." He sounded a little nervous now. "What is this about, again?"

"Did he specify *anything* else about the person? Beyond economic need and academic qualifications?

Such as giving preference to women or minorities?"

"Oh, of course," Dr. Anderson replied, sounding as if he felt he was back on solid ground here. "Dr. Marconi would naturally have preferred to hire a female, a person of color, or someone who was otherwise a member of a marginalized or minority group. He believed in the importance of affirmative action."

"Did he say that specifically?" I asked. "That he preferred to hire a female?"

"Yes."

"Or a minority?"

The professor hesitated. "Yes," he said, with much less certainty. "Of course, much of this would have gone without saying."

"Which part was said, and which part was unsaid?" I asked, wincing as I put him on the spot, hoping this wouldn't somehow get Cherise in trouble.

He paused even longer. "If there's been some kind of complaint, I have heard nothing about it."

"There has been no complaint. It goes to Dr. Marconi's state of mind in his final days, Dr. Anderson. He was a widower who lived alone. Was he hoping for a female employee, or did he give no mention of gender?"

"He preferred a female," the professor finally said, sighing. "He was elderly. He had difficulty walking. I thought... as you said... he's lonely, but surely too old to... what exactly are you asking about here?"

I decided to go ahead and say what was on my

mind. "Are you aware that he left his entire estate to Cherise in his will?" Cherise might get angry at me for revealing this, but I had to gauge the professor's reaction. It was my only chance of knocking loose some crucial detail he was holding back, if any.

The silence on the other end somehow sounded different this time. "He did?" Anderson sounded amazed. "But how? Why? He knew her less than a year. Didn't he have a child at some point?"

"So you can see how there might be questions," I said.

"All kinds of questions. I knew he was estranged from Vera and what's-his-kid, but... yes, I understand. So this isn't a harassment issue, to be clear?"

"Not at all," I said. "In light of that, did he say anything to you to indicate he was looking for an heir or maybe..." My mind blanked annoyingly, my brain fuzzy from lack of sleep, particularly the restful kind where no entities feed on your energy while appearing in the guise of dead relatives. "What's the opposite of a mentor again? If he was the mentor, she'd be—"

"The protégé," he said. "No, he said nothing remotely like that. I can't speak to how he may have seen the relationship in his mind, or how he may have hoped it would develop over time. It sounds as though it worked out quite well for Cherise."

"Yes, I suppose. And you're sure they had no contact before you introduced them regarding this job? They had never met?"

"If they did, they certainly went to a lot of

trouble to hide it from me, and I don't see why they would. My only role was to provide an exchange of contact information. I can't emphasize that enough."

I didn't like prying into my own client's background, but I wouldn't be a detective if I didn't notice that she'd stood to gain more than anyone from Dr. Marconi's death, as long as it looked like a believable accident.

She hadn't wanted to hire us to investigate the house, either; her sister had pushed relentlessly for it. She claimed she hadn't known the professor was going to leave anything to her, and if they hadn't known each other long, she'd certainly had no reason to expect it.

The Cherise-killed-Marconi hypothesis would mean that Piper was mourning the murder of her husband, after all, and Marconi was attacking his own murderer at night by feeding on Cherise. I wasn't sure where Gremel would fit in that scenario, though.

I thanked Dr. Anderson and wrapped up the conversation without my usual bridge-burning move of asking whether he'd heard of any supernatural activities in the house. Cherise had to work with the guy, and I'd already awkwardly blown her cover about the inheritance in my zest to squeeze information out of him.

Then I stepped back in to see Stacey.

"I've got it," she said, beaming.

"What's that?"

"The thing Baron von Jerkin said. Off-hocker. I ran it through some audio translation apps, and it means a stool. Or to squat. Or to pick up."

"Okay," I said. "So he pointed to Cherise's room and told me to... squat?"

"Or to pick up. Maybe like pick up the ghost off of her? Or a stool. Like, hey, pull up a stool and have a look at this."

"I think we're losing something in translation. Send it to my phone and I'll run it by Cherise."

"You're the boss, boss."

Out in the hall again, I looked at the dark doors and considered cutting through the master suite to the library. I wasn't sure how Cherise would feel about seeing me emerge from there, though, so I went the long way, down the front stairs, up the first-floor hall and into the shadowy library.

Chapter Nineteen

Cherise sat at a table in the central library space, the door to the Tomb Room propped open with the same heavy chair. Old volumes were stacked around her. She tapped rapidly at a portable computer, keying information into a database.

"Hi, Cherise?" I said, and she jumped in her chair.

"Sorry," she said. "I was absorbed in the work. And the work is about Byzantine-era incantations for summoning demons and making pacts with them. Not exactly a witty Victorian romance."

"Maybe you could put on some background music to lighten the mood."

"I focus better in silence. What's up? Everything

okay? Are you sleeping in the tent again?"

"I'm undecided. The possibility of random trucks barreling onto the grounds makes it less appealing. But it's nice out there. Fresh air."

"Maybe I should be sleeping outside, too," Cherise said. "If what you said is true. If something in this house is feeding on me while I sleep."

"It didn't respond to the ghost trap, which throws doubt on whether we're dealing with either Dr. or Mrs. Marconi, though it's not conclusive. It's possible the dark cloud is some older entity dredged up by Dr. Marconi's interest in the dark arts. One that preys on people. One that can take on the guise of someone else. My tech manager saw her brother. I... saw my father. You said you weren't having a nightmare when we rudely barged in and woke you up. Do you remember what you were dreaming?"

Cherise looked at me a long moment, then shook her head. "Is this what you came to ask me about?"

"No. Sorry. I mean, yes, that would be helpful to know, but I was hoping you could translate some more German for us."

"Did the talking cold spot have more to say?"

"It did." I played the clip for her.

"*Aufhocker*," she said, frowning.

"Do you know what it means? The translation software just talks about stools and squatting."

"I wouldn't have known before working here." She did a quick search of her own database. "This way."

Unfortunately, but not surprisingly, she went

straight for the Tomb Room, and I followed her
inside.

She'd turned on every lamp, but it did little to
dispel the gloom. The shuttered windows kept the
sunlight out, kept the rows and rows of cluttered
bookshelves above us in shadow. I could imagine
spiders and bats nesting in the upper darkness
among the disorganized volumes and artifacts.

Cherise reached one area of bookshelves where
the old books were neatly organized and labeled by
category. Each shelf was only partly filled, with open
space to accommodate books yet to be cataloged.

She drew on a pair of white linen gloves and
removed an elderly leather volume. Most of these
books had no labels on their spines; a few had
German words I didn't know, while others had
arcane symbols etched into them.

The one she'd selected had a leather cover that
was barely held together by a few dry, meaty strings.
She opened it to a page of dense, handwritten text.
In German, naturally. Strange horned figures in
cloaks and spiky armor adorned the margins of the
books.

"Is this another Johann Gremel book?" I asked.

"No. This is the notebook of an occultist who
lived in eighteenth-century Vlaardingen. It focuses
on classifying spirits and supernatural lore from
around central Europe. Including this one."

She'd turned it to a page with several
illustrations, among scattered, sloping text that
looked hastily scrawled compared to the front page
of the book.

The top of the page was labeled in large, clear letters:

Der Aufhocker.

My eyes flicked quickly among the illustrations. A hooded figure hovered above a drowsy-looking woman, seeming prepared to prey on her. It was featureless, nearly shapeless.

I shivered, looking from the picture to Cherise, thinking of the dark mass that had hovered above her like an oily cloud, feeding on her.

"The aufhocker is a predatory spirit from German folklore," she said, reading over the text. "It preys on weary travelers walking alone at night. It may appear as a friendly fellow traveler at first, or even a friendly animal. Or it may appear as a sad woman."

My eyes went to the second illustration, a weeping woman bent over a cane, her tattered cloak gathered around her as she trudged through the rain. It was hard not to think of the Piper apparitions Aria had seen.

Then I took in the third illustration, a shaggy dark creature with bared teeth.

"The aufhocker can also take the form of a dangerous beast, like a bear or wolf. It can assume many shapes, but originally it is a dead thing, risen from the grave. And it leaps upon the living and drains their energy."

"So it's your basic shapeshifting werewolf vampire zombie ghost," I said.

"Don't forget 'werebear.' Which probably sounds cuter than it should." Cherise shook her head. "Let's hear it again."

"Werebear," I said.

"I meant the recording."

"Oh! Sorry." I replayed the audio clip while she listened closely: *Aufhocker.* "Why did the translation app talk about squatting and stools?" I asked.

"The aufhocker squats atop its victims as it feeds on them." She opened another book, a cheaply bound trade paperback that was nearly falling apart with age. Its age was surely measured in decades and not centuries, and it was definitely not made of parchment and leather.

"Hey, I know that guy," I said, pointing to the cover, which showed a bearded man in a striped stovepipe hat standing in front of Stonehenge. *Dr. Weirdman's Wonderful World of the Weird – Europe Edition!* "Or at least, his great-nephew." Ryan Aberdeen had been a client I'd really clicked with, not much older than me but struggling to raise his kids. His uncle—the pictured "Dr. Weirdman"—had left him an old roadside museum of oddities in Tennessee.

Cherise flipped through some pages about Loch Ness and Dracula's castle, finally landing on a black and white photograph of a fairly creepy statue that appeared to be posted in an otherwise normal and pleasant town square full of sprawling trees and little shops.

The statue was of a man with a walking stick stooped under the weight of a hooded figure perched on his shoulders. The hooded figure gripped him tight and rode him like a horse while glaring down at him with an angry, demonic face.

The caption read: "Aufhocker attacks a traveler; seen in the ancient city of Hildesheim, northern Germany."

"It's hard to believe someone would want to make a statue like that," Cherise said.

"This is what Gremel was trying to tell us," I said. "The entity in this house is an aufhocker. It feeds on the living. It can take on different forms. It's even known for appearing as a sad woman, like we've been seeing."

"I thought the sad woman was his second wife, Piper."

"Right. So..." I tried to pace, but the Tomb Room was far too cluttered. I looked among the strangely decorated bones in their dusty cases, the large wolf skull that watched me from one shelf, the Anubis statue, the small coffin-shaped chest studded with onyx and rubies. That would have been interesting to open, if I'd been willing to move the precariously stacked manuscripts and crumbling old books atop it.

I looked at the round black ritual table covered in candle stumps and mountains of wax. The implements I'd drawn out sat atop it: the ivory and gold dagger he'd used to cut himself as a sacrifice to summon his dead wife, the little golden chalice that had caught the blood, the black crystal sphere he'd used to watch for spirits.

Then I looked over at the open book by Gremel, bound in cracked crocodile leather, the page marked with the long snake tail that had dried and flattened over the years. The elaborate formulae he'd offered for calling up the spirits of the dead, depending on their fate.

"Marconi assumed Piper was an ascended spirit, not wandering or fallen," I said.

"You don't think she was?" Cherise asked. "Who are we to know? I didn't even believe in the afterlife until all of this. Now I don't know what to think."

"But maybe..."

"Maybe she wasn't up there?"

"If the weeping woman is an aufhocker and can appear as different people... then it's possible Marconi never contacted his dead wife's spirit at all." I tapped a drawing in the book, showing a man cutting his wrist and bleeding into a cup, a ghostly figure standing over him, barely noticeable until you stared at the picture long enough. "Maybe this ritual doesn't really draw the souls of lost loved ones down from any higher realm, or from anywhere. Maybe it summons this spirit, this aufhocker, and it feeds on the summoner. It even makes you think it's a dead loved one, coming back to visit you. Like my father."

"Or my mother," Cherise said quietly.

"I'm sorry?" I asked, confused.

"Our mother passed a couple of years ago," she said. "I've been taking care of Aria since then, and it hasn't been easy. Momma had a lot of bills before she died. It was tough. It's still tough. I feel like I'm failing my sister every day. This..." She gestured at the house around her. "This could change everything."

"I'm sorry to hear that. And I can assure you

that you're not failing your sister here. You're not. But what were you saying about your mother?"

"I've been seeing her," she whispered. "Ever since we moved in."

"You've been seeing your mother?"

"Yes. Not all the time. At first, I just thought I heard her footsteps, the way they'd sound when she came in from work at night. I thought I heard them in the library one night. Then another time I thought I heard her voice. Just a few words of 'I Will Survive.' Gloria Gaynor. She used to sing that sometimes, kind of slow and sarcastic, when she was walking out the door to go to work." Cherise removed her glasses and wiped at the corners of her eyes.

"I thought it was my mind playing tricks," she continued. "Then I started seeing her in my room, and in my dreams. She started talking to me. I told myself it was all just dreams.

"Then Aria started telling me about seeing strange things and wanting to do something about it, and I didn't like that idea at all. I'd never believed in the afterlife, like I said, but suddenly I felt my mother was close, and there to help me and guide me, in a way she really hadn't been in a long time. The way she was when I was young, and she always knew what to do."

I nodded. "What kind of advice did she give?"

"She said this was the right place for Aria and me. Said it was a blessing, all arranged from beyond, and I had better hold onto it with both hands."

"Meaning this house?"

"And all the opportunity it represents. I can't let this slip through. I just can't. And she would comfort me, and tell me that as long as I stayed here, I'd be fine."

I nodded. "I told you I saw my father. It's not easy. You want to believe. Just like Marconi wanted to believe he'd summoned Piper. But maybe he didn't do that at all. Does our helpful Dutch occultist have any tips on banishing an aufhocker?"

Cherise checked. "Light, especially sunlight, and the ringing of bells. Church bells are most effective."

"Light and holy music. That's what we use to run spirits off temporarily, but it doesn't defeat them."

"She was summoned by a ritual in Gremel's book," Cherise said, stepping back over to look at the reptile-hide codex again. "Maybe there's something for banishing."

"We can't trust his book. If we're right, then his ritual didn't work. It was a trap for summoning something evil and demonic. Any other rituals in his books could do the same. Plus, based on what I read, we don't want to get involved in these rituals." I shuddered, thinking of the bathtub full of animal guts from which Marconi had summoned the briefly solid—well, liquid—incarnation of his dead wife, or perhaps another entity impersonating her, an aufhocker who specialized in taking on the form of sad weeping women and dead loved ones.

"Then what do we do?"

"Can you translate the Dutch guy's notes on the aufhocker?" I asked.

"I'll do my best."

"Maybe there's something in there we can use." I looked up at the third-story broken railing and window where we'd seen the ghost. "We are going to remove this thing from your house, whatever it takes. I promise you that."

One of the narrow, shadowy walkways above creaked, as though someone had been listening to us and was now walking away, but we saw nobody up there.

Chapter Twenty

"So, the whole time Marconi thought he was sharing his house with the sad ghost of his dead wife, cuddling with her cold spot at night, feeling guilty for ripping her down from heaven—he was actually being fed on by this thing?" Stacey had conjured up the image of the aufhocker statue from the streets of Hildesheim, the dark hooded figure preying on the young man. "It looks like some... giant evil garden gnome. When garden gnomes go bad."

"Gnomes have beards," I said.

"Maybe the ones without beards are evil. That's how you can tell."

We were back in the spare room upstairs. A

drizzle of rain had arrived, making the world outside a cold, dark gray, and completely washing out my level of interest in camping outdoors again. I felt trapped inside the house. And normally, being trapped inside a library on a rainy day sounds great to me, but maybe not this particular library on this particular Saturday.

"So our Piper ghost is a fraud," Stacey said.

"That's one hypothesis."

"Everything's a hypothesis with you. One day you'll be standing at the altar and the preacher will be like 'Do you take this man?' and you'll be like 'That's one hypothesis.'"

"Probably. But yes, it's possible the aufhocker is a demonic entity brought in by a ritual that wasn't what it claimed to be. Gremel's book isn't a reliable source, it turns out."

"But I thought Gremel was helping us."

"His ghost appears to be trying to warn people away from the aufhocker. Especially Aria. I just don't understand why."

"And the shapeshifter hockey thing is treating Aria differently."

"Aufhocker. And yes, it's acting different toward her. Instead of sneaking in and feeding on her when she's drowsy or sleeping, it takes on a crying-woman form that looks like Piper and tries to draw Aria out of the room."

"So the voice we heard in the family cemetery wasn't really Piper?" she asked.

I thought about it—hearing the voice, then seeing the pale girl in the window as we returned. "It seems likely. The aufhocker tries to look nonthreatening at first, like a friendly person or animal, or a helpless and desperate woman. She begged us for help to make us feel bad for her."

"But not very well, because I had to dredge up that audio," Stacey pointed out. "Piper, or the ghost who pretends to be her, is pretty clear when Aria sees her and hears her crying. She was pretty clear when we saw her in the window, too. And Marconi saw her and talked with her a number of times over the years."

"Yeah, good point, Stacey. We wouldn't have seen or heard anything in the cemetery without our equipment. If she was trying to trick us, she wasn't trying very hard. Maybe that one really was Piper's ghost."

"And she was saying, 'help, I don't belong here' because the hockey-offer took her place in the house, pretending to be her, while she's stuck out back in the boneyard with her in-laws. Poor girl."

I chewed on that a minute, sitting on the edge of the bed. Stacey was still looking at the monitors; she still had mountains of footage and other data from the past three nights to sift through. "So, it's possible that neither Philip nor Piper Marconi are haunting this house," I said. "It could just be the aufhocker and Johann Gremel."

"That... would be weird."

"Not as weird as Dr. Weirdman's guide to Europe." I slid the old trade paperback out of my bag. The glue holding the book together had crumbled over the years, and many of the pages were loose.

"You're kidding!" She opened to the bookmarked page and looked at the aufhocker statue, the same one that she'd already found on her phone. Dr. Weirdman's picture was taken a little closer, a little more focused on the thing's creepy, goblin-like face. "There it is. The ugly critter we're looking for. From this angle it kind of looks like an evil Smurf."

"Hopefully we can catch it before it can harm our clients."

"You mean, 'hopefully we can smurf it before it smurfs our smurfs.'"

"Any word from Jacob?"

"He's coming. It'll be late this afternoon. Tax season, you know. A busy time of year for psychics. If they daylight as accountants."

"We're lucky he's willing to come at all, as far out as we are."

"Yep, he's pretty dream-tastic." Stacey frowned out at the drizzling rain. "I was thinking of running into town for lunch and snacking materials, but it's so yuck out there. Good thing I've got more granola bars."

"We ought to have something better to offer when he gets here. We can't have our psychic bleeding from the roof of his mouth."

"Are you insulting my Stoneground bars?"

"Well, they definitely live up to their name, since they taste like rocks covered in dirt." I took one from our diminishing supply. It was labeled Triple Nut Flavor; I was pretty sure at least some of those nuts were acorns. With shell.

We slept in shifts that afternoon, one person staying awake to guard the other one who slept. We monitored the room for temperature and electromagnetic fluctuations that could indicate the aufhocker had returned to feed on us. A thermal camera in the hall watched for cold spots in case the entity wanted to go after Cherise or Aria instead. Both of them retreated to their rooms for part of their Saturday, presumably to rest after the previous night's action.

I took the second sleeping shift—so when the screaming began, it woke me up. Fortunately, I'd been having one of my usual nightmares instead of a pleasant aufhocker-induced dream about a dead relative, so I wasn't completely drained when I pushed myself out of bed to follow the screams.

I was disoriented, though, as I ran out the door and down the hall, barefoot, not taking the time to strap on my boots or utility belt. I did bring a flashlight, though. Stacey ran at my side.

The screaming came from Cherise's room down the hall. Her door was closed, but thankfully not locked, so we rushed right in.

Cherise was sitting up, clawing at the air in front of her, looking like she was fighting something invisible while struggling to catch her breath.

We clicked on the overhead lights and flooded the room with our own high-powered, full-spectrum flashlights.

Cherise screamed again. The blankets and pillows had been stripped from her bed. She slid backwards across the mattress, propelled by an unseen force, until her back slammed into the headboard.

Stacey played the music she'd downloaded earlier after we'd learned about the aufhocker. It was a playlist of church bells collected from cathedrals around Germany, largely by bell enthusiasts who'd recorded them and posted them free online. Apparently bell enthusiasts exist.

I winced as the inside of the room turned into a clanging, clonging belfry. If the holiness of the bells didn't drive the spirit away, maybe they would at least annoy it into leaving.

Rushing to Cherise's side, I grabbed her hand and shoved my light into the space in front of her, though I still didn't see anything there.

Cherise clung to me, gasping for air, but not screaming or clawing anymore.

"Are you okay?" I asked her. "Can you breathe? Can you speak?"

She nodded. "Yeah."

"Let's get out of here." I helped her to her feet. She winced as if in pain, but had no trouble walking out to the hall with me.

Stacey remained in the room until we'd left, then hurried out and slammed the door behind her. Her clanging bells kept pealing out from the speaker on her belt, and I motioned for her to dampen it down a little before my skull cracked from the noise.

She turned it way down, leaving the bells as a kind of atmospheric background, like a church announcing the time in a distant village. And never stopping.

"What happened?" I asked Cherise, who held tight to my arm.

"It was him," she said, and she winced again. "He was on top of me. Crushing down."

"Who?" I asked, thinking of the dark cloud. It had usually taken the form of her mother, hadn't it?

"Marconi," she whispered. She cleared her throat. "Dr. Marconi. He was on me, and it felt like he was trying to... get inside me. Here." She loosened a button on her frayed pajama top to show me.

Three bright red scratches ran from the top of her shoulder to her chest, like something had tried to claw out her heart. Or claw its way in.

"That looks painful," Stacey said. "We've got a first aid kit."

"Wait, it was the dead professor this time?" I asked. "This is his first appearance, isn't it? We haven't seen him. Neither has Aria."

We all looked up the hall to Aria's door, still firmly shut. Despite the screaming and the insanely loud bells, she hadn't stepped out to investigate.

A worried look passed among us, and we bolted toward her door.

Cherise got there first, despite her recent injuries, and pounded with both fists.

She screamed her sister's name, but no response came from within. She tried opening the door, but it wouldn't budge.

"Aria!" she shouted, kicking the door repeatedly. "Aria, answer me!"

No answer came.

"Let me try." I drew back and stomped the door with the sole of my boot, the way my mostly retired boss Calvin Eckhart had taught me, presumably the same way the Savannah Police Department had taught him.

The door was old, which unfortunately meant it was thicker and more solid than the interior doors of most modern homes. It took several stomps just to crack it, several more to actually bust it open and send it swinging inward. If only my kickboxing instructors back home could see me now.

When the door opened, I charged into the room with my flashlight drawn, Stacey close behind me, Cherise right behind her.

Aria sat at the antique rolltop desk with her back toward us, a math book open in front of her, wearing huge earphones that completely swallowed her ears.

She spun around with a shock on her face as I charged toward her, her broken door swinging wide behind me.

"What are you doing?" She lifted one earphone, unleashing a storm of brassy old-time jazz music. She looked to her sister, who'd charged in right behind us. "What's happening?"

"I saw him," Cherise said.

"Who?" Aria removed her headphones and jumped to her feet. "The skeleton guy? Why's my door broken?"

"Because you weren't *answering* it," Cherise said.

"Did you consider *texting* me?" Aria held up her phone.

"I was distracted." She pulled her pajama shirt aside to reveal the scratches.

Aria gaped while Cherise told her what she'd seen. Stacey grabbed antibiotic cream and bandages for the scratches.

"I don't think you should stay in this house anymore, Aria," Cherise said. "You have to leave."

The timbers of the house let out a low moan below, as if protesting this statement.

"We both have to leave," Aria said. "That's what I've been saying this whole time. This place is bad. Just bad."

"I can't. I need this job."

"You're kidding. Even after that?" Aria pointed to the scratched area over Cherise's heart, now covered again by the flannel.

"I can't give up on this," Cherise said.

"Even if it kills you?" Aria asked. "Because that's what happened to the last guy who lived in this house, didn't it? It killed him. That library is full of evil things, and you know it."

"Maybe you both should pack up and stay at a hotel tonight," I said. "Our psychic will be here soon to help us investigate. It may stir things up. I don't want to see either of you get hurt."

"We can't move out," Cherise repeated.

"It's just for tonight. There's a very inexpensive motel outside Athens—"

"—where you don't want to stay," Stacey hurried to add. "Pay the extra ten bucks for the Holiday Inn Express or whatever, trust me."

"I'll be ready in ten minutes," Aria announced,

grabbing a small suitcase from under her bed and then grabbing clothes from her dresser. "Why aren't you getting packed, Cherise?"

Cherise still looked undecided.

"I'll help you," I offered. "Stacey, you stick with Aria. We don't leave either of them alone until they're packed and in the car."

"This feels like a bad idea," Cherise said, after I'd steered her out to the hallway as gently as I could. We started toward her room. "You don't think any harm will come to the library while I'm gone, do you?"

"I wouldn't think so," I said, a little confused by her priorities at the moment, considering she'd just been attacked by one of the library's resident ghosts.

"Good." As we reached her room, she lowered her voice. "If you get rid of the bad one, does that mean I won't see my mother again? Awake or asleep?"

"Well," I began, which was just a placeholder word, because I wasn't sure exactly how to navigate this treacherous-sounding emotional minefield. "The aufhocker is a deceptive ghost. It pretended to be Stacey's brother, and my father—"

"I know, I know," Cherise hurried to interrupt, as though she didn't want to hear me spell it out again. "I know it's not *really* her. But I was almost getting used to seeing her again. Sometimes I just hear her voice in the library, or smell her perfume when I'm lying asleep at night, and it comforts me. When I see her out of the corner of my eye, or dream about her, it feels like she's back, stronger and wiser than ever, ready to protect us and guide us, instead of all that being on my shoulders now. How do I guide my sister when I'm only a step or two ahead on the path, and I don't know where any of it leads? The responsibility's exhausting. Being alone with no help is exhausting. At school, I'm surrounded by people my own age whose biggest fear is which keg party they're attending this weekend. And I'm over here trying not to wreck Aria's life permanently through some mistake or oversight while also trying figure out how not to wreck my own."

"I'm sorry," I said, sort of awkwardly patting her shoulder. I'm not the greatest at this kind of thing. "But you definitely have to understand—"

"When I thought my mother was watching over us, I felt like there was hope. Like there was a plan. And like I said, I didn't believe in anything, spiritually, before we moved to this house. My mother did, and my grandmother, but I just couldn't bring myself to have faith. There's so much suffering, so many horrors inflicted by people on people... I don't know. It's almost better to believe there's nothing out there than to believe there's some all-powerful being who just watches it all. Just watches and lets it happen.

"But since moving here," Cherise continued, "sure, maybe I've felt overwhelmed, but I felt like I wasn't alone. Like I can feel my mother's hand on the wheel, invisible but helping me steer."

I felt worse for her with every word she spoke, and also like we were getting mired in quicksand. I wanted to get her and Aria out of the house for the night, and Cherise had made little progress. She'd taken a suitcase out of the closet and put it on the bed, but hadn't even begun to pack it.

I chose my words carefully. You'd think a degree in psychology would have made me better with people, but its main effect was helping me question my own sanity all the time. I'd gone to Armstrong State, a local college that was itself now a ghost, its pirate flags lowered forever as it became an appendage of Georgia Southern University.

"This sounds exactly like what Dr. Marconi described in his journal," I said, and Cherise flinched a little, likely because a phantom of the dead professor had just attacked her in bed. "He believed the aufhocker was his deceased wife. At first he was happy just to have her around again. He kept trying to take comfort from her, to connect with her, to please her and make her stronger.

"But she was tricking him. She fed on him like a parasite. Like that goblin creature riding on the traveler's back, wearing him down with every step. No matter how much he gave her, it was never enough. It was never going to be enough. Marconi was stuck inside the house with her like a fly in a pitcher plant. Until he died."

Cherise stiffened. "Do you suppose he finally figured out the aufhocker wasn't really his dead wife, so it killed him? Pushed him to his death in the library?"

"That's possible. And it's another argument for getting you and your sister out now. Because now you know the truth. You know the aufhocker is not really your mother. You still have the chance to do what Marconi failed to do, and get free."

"But who will take care of the library?" she asked.

"You're concerned about that?"

"Of course. The collection may be strange, but it contains a number of extremely rare and completely unique items. Some of these books are centuries old. There are pieces of parchment that could be more than a thousand years old. This collection can't just be abandoned."

I nodded along, finding it hard to disagree. "But you can't live here anymore. And you can't be alone here anymore. You'll want to work with bright, full-spectrum lights and with sacred music in the background."

"Like those bells?" She grimaced.

"Anything of your choice," I replied. "It can help keep the negative spirits at bay. We can talk about all this later. Right now, we need to get your sister to a safe place. You don't want Dr. Marconi trying to claw his way inside her next."

Cherise looked shocked, then disgusted, by what I said, but it jolted her into action and she finally started packing in earnest, flying around the room to grab her things.

"You're right," she told me. "I know. I shouldn't get drawn in by this... this mirage. I should have told you from the beginning. I should have been honest with Aria when she told me about seeing strange things. But I'm not going to persist in error. I'm getting my sister out of here."

Another long, strange groan sounded from the depths of the house. The shutters rattled, as if a stiff wind blasted them from outside. It didn't sound like a Ford F150 this time.

Strange rumbling echoed down the hallway.

I stepped out, and so did Stacey, and together we looked toward the end of the hall, in the direction of the sound.

The heavy double doors to the master suite creaked and pushed toward us as though someone were shoving them outward, straining against the lock. Trying to escape. Trying to reach us.

The movement stopped... then started back stronger and harder, rattling the doors in their frame, as if someone had shoved against the lock in frustration.

"What now?" Aria asked, stepping out of her room beside Stacey. Cherise emerged, too. Cherise and I were much closer to the doors.

Then the thick doors slammed and bulged as though some giant wild animal had crashed into them from behind, trying to break free, trying to get to us.

Aria screamed.

The doors still didn't open. Both knobs began rattling as if hands gripped them on the inside and shook them.

"Let's go!" I told Cherise.

Before she could even reach into the bedroom to grab her suitcase, a loud splintering crack sounded.

The doors flew open like black curtains. A

howling gale of icy wind filled the hallway, blowing my hair back, biting through my clothes and deep into my bones.

We screamed.

Ahead, the darkness of the inner corridor was complete, every light extinguished. There wasn't much light from the glass balcony doors behind us, either, because the sun had set.

It was like staring into an abyss.

Rattling, clacking noises sounded within.

I pointed my flashlight into the darkness.

The pictures on the wall trembled as if an earthquake shook them, though I could feel no such vibrations. Images of Philip as a promising young professor, of Piper as a promising and even younger dancer, wobbled on the walls, shimmering as my flashlight reflected off their frames.

Then, one by one, the pictures began to fall like glass raindrops, shattering as they struck the floor on either side of the hall.

At the far end of the hall, the next pair of heavy doors blew open, revealing the library's honeycomb of walkways, ladders, and bookshelves. It felt like an invitation—into darkness, madness, and death.

"It's like the house wants us to go into the library," Cherise whispered.

"So we're heading out the front door instead. Come on." I started toward the stairs, as did Stacey. Aria was already ahead of us, standing on the top stair with her suitcase.

Cherise continued staring down the dark hallway, past the falling and shattering pictures into the library.

"I notice you're not moving," I said to Cherise, stopping to look back. "Can you grab your suitcase?"

"I have to go in there," she murmured.

I thought she meant the bedroom where her suitcase was, but no. She started toward the master suite and the library beyond.

"That's a really bad idea," I said.

"My purse is in the library," she said. "Car keys, credit card, everything I'd need to get out of here and head to a hotel."

I sighed. "All right. Go head out front with Stacey and Aria. I'll grab the purse and catch up with you."

Stacey looked torn when I told her we had to split up, but somebody had to stick with the clients and somebody had to go in and face the risk. We couldn't leave the clients alone or take them deeper into danger with us.

"Just hurry. I'll see you out there." Stacey gave me a quick hug and headed down the front stairs with Cherise and Aria.

I grabbed my jacket, belt, and boots, then started down the hallway alone.

The atmosphere grew noticeably colder and thicker as I passed through the first set of double doors and into the master suite.

Low whispers sounded behind the suite's closed doors. Strange, high laughter pealed from behind the bathroom door where Marconi had once raised a ghastly incarnation of Piper from animal blood and guts.

I chose not to open that particular door.

Then I stepped out of the master suite and onto the intersection of narrow second-story walkways in the dark library.

Directly ahead, but a story above, was the broken railing where Marconi had died and the window where we'd spotted the apparition of Piper. Our thermal camera and microphone were still up there; we hadn't even begun to study that data.

The library was completely dark, the light switch unresponsive.

The sights my flashlight found were bizarre. It was hard to wrap my mind around what I was seeing.

Books had been arranged in strange, nearly impossible configurations. Spiral columns of old books towered more than two stories high, stacked carefully, their hard leather covers barely overlapping each other. These tall columns were precariously balanced on the edges and corners of tables below; some even stood on the seats of the library's chairs.

Archways of books spanned from one wall to another across the open spaces of the library's second and third levels, enormous curves like the ribs of whales or dinosaurs.

It was hard to see how it could have been accomplished; the books were crammed in cover to cover, pressed tightly together, defying gravity. Hundreds of books made up every arch.

The spirits in the house were definitely acting out, and the particular way they were expressing themselves gave me the chills. There was intelligence and focus here, in addition to the physical power to move all these objects in a short amount of time.

It had to have been arranged quickly, all at once, because the books were all holding each other up. I thought of the hundred-handed giants of Greek mythology who guarded the defeated elder gods in the underworld.

I remembered Cherise's suspicion that the aufhocker had turned against Marconi after he'd determined that it wasn't actually the ghost of his wife. Maybe the aufhocker had been listening to us and knew we'd figured things out. It didn't want to lose the people it had been preying on. With no residents in the house, it would go hungry.

Cherise's purse waited atop the table in the center of the first floor where she'd been working. The strange columns and arches of books swayed all around and above it.

I adjusted my flashlight to flood mode, but deep gloom still shrouded the immense space. Solid darkness lay beyond my small, moving oasis of light.

The nearest staircase felt more fragile and unstable than ever as I descended it. Each narrow step creaked and groaned like rotten plywood.

Clearly, one of the spirits had been quite psychokinetically busy in here. If it could stack and arrange thousands of books into these insanely elaborate and delicately balanced arches and columns, there was no telling what else it could do.

Maybe that was the purpose of this elaborate display—to show power, to instill fear. Perhaps the necromancer himself, the dead professor, was angry at us for investigating his old house and invading the forbidden area of his private rooms.

The staircase, despite its profuse creaking and groaning, did not snap beneath me. I reached the first floor and approached the center table.

I couldn't help trembling as I crossed under the arches of books. They were like enormous sprawling tentacles above.

It felt like some invisible giant had been at play here, and maybe still was, though the room was completely silent at the moment.

The cold, thick air only grew colder and thicker as I approached the table holding Cherise's purse and laptop. My nerves urged me to run, but I didn't dare. I could easily brush against a column of books and bring everything crashing down around me.

My heart thumped as I finally reached the table. Three of the weird book arches came together here, meeting atop a precarious column of books at one corner of the table. There were hundreds of books altogether, barely holding each other aloft in a complex configuration that made me think of a giant spider waiting to pounce on its prey.

I closed the laptop, slid it into its case, and slid the strap over my shoulder. Then, trembling even harder, I picked up the purse. It sat directly next to the precarious column of heavy leather books, nearly touching it.

As I lifted her purse, her car keys jangled inside.

I noticed something else on the table: the other ring of keys, the ones that came with the house. I could use those.

As I lifted the key ring from the table, a slow,

leathery hiss sounded from above.

I pointed my flashlight at the arch of books above my head.

A single book was sliding loose—just one book, moving so slowly it was almost imperceptible, inching its way free.

I turned to run, but I wasn't fast enough.

That one book fell loose, dropped straight down, and landed with a hard thump on the floor beside me.

On its own, it would have been innocuous.

Under the circumstances, though, it was like the detonator on a bomb.

The archway of books seemed to exhale and ripple, every tightly pressed-together volume separating slightly from the books on either side of it.

Then all the books came crashing down. Heavy volumes struck me with bruising force again and again as I ran toward the dark doors at the front of the library.

A column of books came down and broke across my back, their spines smashing into my own. The impact knocked me over. My stomach came down on the long edge of the laptop bag, and the laptop's hard edge jabbed into my guts.

I let out a fairly audible "oof!" as I sprawled forward onto my face. Stupid laptop.

More columns of books fell, one after another, a collapsing city of paper towers. I was still under attack.

There was a heavy groan as the dark doors ahead

began to move. They were closing, moved by unseen hands, with me still sprawled on the floor inside. I was going to be trapped.

I struggled to my feet as the avalanche of books came down around me. Binding shattered; loose pages and broken covers spread everywhere. I felt bad for the damage to all the old books, but couldn't help feeling a bit less so after so many of them had attacked me.

I barely made it through the library doors before they slammed together.

Ahead, the house's heavy front doors had been propped open for my benefit by Stacey and Cherise, but the doors were straining against their built-in doorstops, trying to snap shut as I ran toward them up the front hall.

They snapped loose and slammed shut just as I raced through them out to the portico.

Stacey and Cherise were standing on the gravel driveway and turned their heads at the sound of the slamming front doors. Aria sat in Cherise's car, drumming her fingers, waiting to go.

More headlights approached from the desolate road behind them as I hurried past the column Vic had smashed with his truck and down the front steps.

When I was clear of the house, I stopped to catch my breath. I was glad to be out of danger for the moment, but our work was far from over.

Chapter Twenty-One

"Everything okay?" Stacey asked, probably picking up on subtle cues, such as the panicked look on my face and the way I'd bolted out the front door like demons were on my heels.

"Definitely not," I said, watching the approaching headlights.

A gray Hyundai pulled into the weedy drive, tires crunching on gravel, and parked alongside our old blue van.

"Jacob!" Stacey dashed over to greet him as he climbed out of the car, looking worn down from his drive, his hair mussed and his business-casual clothes rumpled. He barely had time to adjust his glasses before Stacey leaped onto him and kissed him; his energetic blonde girlfriend pouncing on him seeming to improve his mood.

I greeted him in a more reserved and professional fashion.

"Sorry I'm late," he said. "Do you want to hear the details of this particular shipping company's tax issues, or can we stipulate that my job is boring and no one cares?"

"I'm all about some stipulation, baby," Stacey said, clinging to him a bit longer before backing away, apparently remembering that our clients hadn't driven off yet. She downshifted to a more professional tone. "So, uh, this is the house. The subject of our investigation."

"Really interesting," he said, looking it over. Jacob had been given no information about the new case, so he could approach it with fresh eyes. He was an extremely reluctant medium, his powers having awoken fairly abruptly after a near death experience in an airplane crash. He was an accountant by day, and his psychic powers seemed to annoy him more than anything. "I'm already picking up a lot."

"Maybe we shouldn't start in the main house," I suggested, having just fled it and not eager to go right back inside to see what awaited us there. "How about we check the cemetery first?"

"Oh, yeah!" Stacey said, then covered her mouth so she didn't say anything about the voice we'd recorded there. "Good idea. Let's get that out of that way," she added through her fingers.

"Are you going to be okay?" I asked Cherise.

"Sure." She was looking at her phone, trying to

get a signal, while Aria sat in the car, still drumming her fingers and staring impatiently at her. "I'll find us a hotel. Are you sure it's safe for y'all in there?"

"We'll be fine," I said, though I had my doubts. "You just drive safe and find somewhere pleasant to stay."

Then we piled into the van and drove the short distance down to the cemetery road, where we again pulled in just enough to park.

"Do you want to go with flashlights or night vision goggles?" I asked Jacob.

"Better keep it simple and stick with flashlights," he said, and Stacey passed him one.

"Keep them dim," I said. "We don't want to run off any entities that might be around."

We climbed out and headed up the road, stepping over fallen limbs from the low canopy above.

"The overgrown road to the backwoods graveyard, huh?" he said, looking around as we passed through the woods. "Sounds cheerful. Like a walk through Candyland."

"We don't have to stay long," I said. It was hard making conversation while not telling him anything about the case. I hadn't had a chance to fill Stacey in on all that had gone down inside the house, and it was hard not to talk about that, either.

We fell silent, listening to the sounds of the thick woods as we walked, the scuttling and whispering sounds of the many hidden inhabitants.

I unlocked the gate, the heavy old house keys clacking together loudly in the quiet night.

The gate creaked open, the noise sharp and piercing. It felt like it would draw unwanted attention somehow. We weren't illegally trespassing, but I couldn't say the old burial ground had a warm and welcoming feeling. I definitely felt like we were unwanted intruders.

"It must be convenient having your own cemetery right in your back yard," Jacob said, looking among the tombstones, his eyes naturally drawn to the large monument to Philip and Piper. "It's like having the past and the future right in front of you all the time. So, there's definitely some low-level residual energy around here, too, but... uh... what?" Jacob was suddenly staring off into seemingly empty space beyond the big dark marble slab, seeing something I wasn't.

He stared for a long while, blinking and shaking his head, Stacey nudged him.

"I can't understand her," he muttered. Then, louder, looking ahead into the cold darkness, he said, "I'm sorry. You have to slow down. I'm catching every fifth word here."

"What are you seeing?" I asked.

"There's a girl here. Not a residual, either. She's *here*. Talking so fast the lower part of her face is all blurred." He turned his gaze back to the emptiness. "Yeah, again, you'll have to slow down. I can't understand anything."

"What does she look like? Aside from the blurry motormouth?"

"She's young, like maybe a teenager," he said. "Brownish hair, freckles. Died fairly recently, considering how old this house and cemetery are."

"How can you tell she's recent?"

"Well, her apparition is strong and clear, not a faded echo. Also, she's wearing one of those Nirvana shirts with the x'ed-out eyes, so she can't possibly go back any earlier than the 1990s, but probably even more recent."

"You're quite the Encyclopedia Brown on that one," Stacey said.

"I would get you more details if she would *slow down* to a pace that actual humans can understand." Jacob closed his eyes. "She's speaking in images instead of words. Her memories, it's so awkward when they just give you their memories... she's walking down the street, past big brick buildings with white columns. She's wearing a backpack, going to class, coming from class. Students flood the sidewalks and the streets around her. Headphones on. Twenty One Pilots playing. Everything seems to move in time with the music. All right, so... oh. Later, much later. Same street, but dark and deserted. No music."

Jacob walked with his eyes closed past the handful of grave markers to the open grassy area beyond, presumably the site of future graves.

"She's sick. Stumbling. Too much to drink. She's never had a drink before. And she's lost. She's a freshman. All the buildings are unfamiliar. Where did her roommate go? She's wandering through campus alone. It's very late, she doesn't know how late. She's full of regret and guilt and starting to panic.

"Headlights on the road. They slow down. She's

worried it's the police, but it's not. Just an old man, looks like a professor. He seems friendly, frail, non-threatening. Offers her a ride.

"At some point, she realizes the car ride's gone on much too long. She couldn't have been this far from her dorm. Now there's no town in sight. There's nothing, it's all dark. She panics, he tries to soothe her. That doesn't work, so he jabs her with something painful and bright. Electrical. Then she's out.

"Her next memory is waking up in a dark place. There." Jacob opened his eyes and pointed in the direction of the house, though we couldn't see it through the woods. "She wants us to go there. She has something to show us."

I glanced at Stacey. Brown hair, freckles? Nirvana t-shirt? It didn't sound like Piper, but it didn't sound like anyone else we'd heard about, either.

"I am so confused," Stacey whispered to me.

"Oh, I don't mean she woke up right there in the woods," Jacob said, apparently thinking she'd been talking to him. "Back at the house."

"The house is a little messy," I told him. "And potentially dangerous. I can be more specific if you want—"

"Not yet. Just tell me to duck if a ghost throws an ax at my head, that kind of thing."

"What else are you picking up around here?" I asked.

"Nirvana Girl is pretty much the star attraction," Jacob said.

"Can you ask her name?"

"What's your... yeah, I can't understand that. She's just squeaking. Talking much too fast. Slow down! She's not slowing. This is one chatty dead girl. Probably was chatty in life, hasn't had anyone to talk to since... well, since they buried her. Right here." He pointed at a weedy patch of the open, not-yet-used area of the cemetery.

"With no marker?" Stacey asked.

"Exactly. Why would they do that?" Jacob turned and looked past us, up the path toward the gate. "She's waiting for us over there. She wants us to go up to the house with her."

"Yeah, I thought I felt an extra chill pass through me," Stacey said. "Come on, Nirvana Girl, don't walk through me again, okay? It's weird."

The three of us—four, counting our invisible dead companion—left through the cemetery gate, deliberately leaving it open. Closing it might have caused the cemetery to reclaim her in some way, and we couldn't have our nameless surprise witness vanishing back into her grave.

Dry leaves crunched as we walked. At times, I thought I could hear extra footsteps beside me, but I resisted the temptation to turn and look, worried my glance might send the ghost flying away into the night like a startled bird.

As we approached the bend in the road where we could see the back of the house in the distance, Stacey and I slowed to look through the break in the trees.

The same window glowed again, the same pale

blonde girl looking down at us. Her eerie glow vanished with a faint cracking sound, though it must have been fairly loud if it reached us.

"I just saw something in that window." Jacob pointed.

"We all saw something in that window," Stacey said. "But thanks for playing."

"It was watching us. It was... brrr. Even the other ghost caught a chill off that one, I think. Its gaze was ice cold. That's no typical ghost up there, is it?"

"It does appear atypical," I said, trying to keep it vague. And succeeding, I think.

We crunched onward through the chilly, shadowy woods.

"Is she still walking with us?" I asked Jacob as we approaching the van.

"Yes, but I don't see her hopping in the van," Jacob said. "Especially since getting into a stranger's car didn't exactly pay off for her last time."

"Okay. Stacey, take the van. We'll meet you at the house." I passed her the keys.

She climbed in and backed the van into the road, careful not to turn on the headlights until they were pointed away from us.

I couldn't help feeling a moment of unease watching her drive off, leaving us alone on an abandoned road with a strange spirit we'd just escorted out of the cemetery. Now who was doing necromancy?

"Which way does she want to go?" I asked Jacob.

"Right through the rusty barbed wire fence," he said. "Not really that considerate of the living."

We helped each other over the fence without getting spiked or gored, so that was an accomplishment. Then it was a matter of walking through high weeds, over ground still bumpy with the memory of furrows from when the place had been a working farm long ago.

"Watch out for that rock," Jacob said, right as I tripped over it. He caught me before I could sprawl onto my face. Too bad he hadn't been in the library earlier.

We crossed the overgrown field. Occasionally the moon and stars glowed down on us for a moment or two, only to be obscured by clouds again, leaving us with just our flashlights to guide us.

"This house you're investigating has serious issues," he said. "You've probably picked up on that by now."

"Something attacked us right before we came out," I told him. "So, yep. Active haunting. With a big side dish of serious emotional issues."

"It amazes me that you keep going into places like this, after all you've been through inside of them."

"You've been through plenty of it with us."

"True. I mean, ever the since the crash, I've had to deal with the dead. Sometimes they follow me home and harass me when I'm trying to sleep.

"One time I was in a meeting at work, the clients over here and the senior partner over there, and one of the company's founders was standing over in the corner trying to get involved. Ben Ewanowski. He'd been dead almost a year, died at his desk at age ninety-one. He'd died on an April sixteenth, the day after tax season ended.

"Anyway, he was such a workaholic that he hung around a couple years after he died, still trying to manage his biggest client engagements, issuing instructions to staff members who couldn't hear him.

"Being ignored fueled his temper, which hadn't been that great in life. He'd go on these angry tirades nobody but me ever heard. Sometimes he'd lash out and a book would fall mysteriously from a shelf or papers would slide off a table. And I'd have to sit there and pretend I was as clueless as everyone else, because talking to invisible people at work can have a negative effect on one's career."

"I do it all the time," I said.

"Different career path," he said.

"I can't recommend mine. The pay varies widely by case, and sometimes it's a long wait between good checks."

"Never mind the money; seeing the dead and fighting the dangerous ones only made me appreciate the logic and predictability of accounting. It went from a safe but boring job to a *refreshingly* safe and boring job compared to what I do with you and Stacey."

"You've help a lot," I said. "Even if you're only a weekend warrior against evil."

"Accountants fight evil, too," he said. "Untidy records. Wasteful expenditures."

"I forgot about the exciting wasteful expenditures."

"They're everywhere, often invisible, and can be very draining. Just like ghosts."

"I can't tell whether you're making your job sound interesting or mine sound boring. Here's the next barbed wire fence. Who wants to go first?"

We managed to climb over more barbed wire without any slashing, stabbing, or tetanus-inducing incidents.

Stacey waited for us by the van, pacing and kicking gravel, clearly impatient. The house was completely dark, no sign of electrical life inside. Cherise's car was gone.

"Took y'all long enough," she said. "What's the plan, Ellie?"

"What does Nirvana Girl say?" I asked Jacob.

"She's actually hanging by the fence." He pointed back the way we'd come. "She's afraid to come any closer."

"Why?" Stacey asked. "I mean, she's already dead, what's the worst that can happen?"

"I don't know, but she's not budging. She's just nodding and kind of hopping around. She wants us to go in. Even though she refuses to."

I looked toward the fence, but saw no sign of the girl. "Oh, come on," I said. "Easy for her to say."

"She's showing me images of books, lots of books. A library. She wants us to go the library?" Jacob rubbed his head. "Now I'm confused. Did she die with a book checked out or something? She can't move on until she clears up her overdue fines?"

"This house is at least seventy percent library," Stacey said. "She probably just means to go inside."

"Oh." Jacob looked at the big temple-like house with new interest. "Sounds cool."

"You're such a box of Nerds," Stacey said. "Actually, I wish we had some candy right now."

"We have plenty of Stoneground bars left," I said. "We should just chuck those at the ghost."

"Not even the dead could survive that," Jacob agreed.

"Whatever, they're stuffed with nutrients and good times," Stacey said. "That's the Stoneground Pledge."

I looked at the dark front doors, last seen slamming themselves to trap me inside, with more than a little apprehension. We were probably all feeling it, hence the desperate joking. I was worried about leading my friends in there to face the dangerous entity inside, but it was up to us to deal with it, to protect Cherise and Aria like we protected all of our clients. The money was terrible, but the work was a powerful calling.

"Okay," I said. "It's hazardous in there, so let's load up."

We grabbed backpacks from the van and filled them with gear. I hung my thermal goggles around my neck in case I needed them. Though called goggles, they don't much resemble the little plastic things for swimming; they're more like a solid heavy brick that affixes fairly unpleasantly to one's face.

Once we were ready, the three of us ascended the stairs to the portico. Jacob pointed at the damaged column with some concern.

"Did a ghost do that?"

"It was a Ford F-150," Stacey said.

"Someone should probably get that fixed." He turned toward the door again. "There's nobody home, correct?"

"Nobody alive." I opened the door and stepped inside.

"Well, that's a pleasant way to describe it." He walked in, passing the flashlight over the bookshelves in the high entrance hall. These hadn't been rearranged crazily like the ones in the actual library. "Do they have lights in this place?"

I flipped the switch on the wall. Nothing happened. "Looks like we're stuck with darkness. Sorry."

"At least it's warmer than a freezer in here," he said. "But not by much. Colder inside than outside, that's never good..."

He explored, looking into the parlor lined with classic texts, the dining room with its immense dark slab of a table, where we hadn't spent much time. He looked around the kitchen, investigated the pantry, found a twelve-pack of lunch-sized Fritos, ripped one open and snacked on it.

"Not bad," he said. "Haven't had these in a while."

He opened the cellar door by the kitchen, and we went down. It wasn't a full basement, more like a walled-off area with some shelves and a floor among the brick foundations of the house. It looked like a storage place for forgotten old jars full of forgotten old funk, plus scattered rusty hand tools on a mildewed bench.

"I see this is where they kept their old-time cobweb collection," Jacob said. He walked to one wall, frowning. "Is this the whole cellar? There's nothing else down here?"

"It looks like this is it," I said. "We haven't really gone under the house."

"The clients didn't report any activity down here?" Jacob asked. He sounded a little perplexed.

"I'm not sure the clients ever came down here at all," I said.

"Yeah, who would?" Stacey asked, grimacing at the strange dirty jars that her flashlight couldn't penetrate.

"Are you picking up something, Jacob?"

"Maybe. It's faint." He looked at the wall and shook his head. "Let's keep going."

Next, we headed upstairs to check the bedrooms before entering the library. The entities in the house were laying low so far, but I figured entering the library might provoke them again.

Upstairs, we kept our flashlights off, depending on the pale light through the glass balcony doors and the windows.

"There's some activity here, but it would be hard not to guess that based on all your equipment." He stood in the middle of the hallway and turned his head slowly, like it was some kind of radar dish taking readings. Sometimes I don't know if he's serious with this stuff or playing it up.

He extended his arms. Closed his eyes. Wiggled his fingers.

He looked in at the bedrooms, but was mainly

interested in the *Magicia* books on the shelves.

"Wow, this is a rare edition," he said. "Check out those swamp dragons."

"Put it back," I said.

Finally, we ended up back in the front hall after he'd walked through all the front bedrooms.

"No reason to go anywhere except dead ahead." Jacob pointed at the dark doors.

"Dead ahead? In a haunted house?" Stacey asked him. "So funny."

"What? That joke killed at the Winchester House."

"I know entire dads who wouldn't laugh at that." Stacey's face went serious, though, as she looked at the dark doors, probably remembering how they'd bulged and flown open, the lock breaking, the icy air filling the hallway. Now the doors stood partially open, and it was hard not to imagine something watching us from the darkness within.

Inside, the length of hallway was filled with shattered glass. Only a few pictures remained on the wall, all of them askew, some flipped backwards.

"Looks like good times ahead." Jacob stopped only a few paces into the master suite. "Yeah, this place is definitely active. The entity here is an older man, very strong energy. Much stronger than the typical active ghost. He's territorial, like this is definitely his house, or at least it is now. He spends a lot of time in here." Jacob opened the master bedroom door.

The heavy curtains around the bed rustled, as though something moved inside them.

"He doesn't like any of us being here," Jacob said. "He looks old and frail... oh, but now he's showing himself as young and handsome."

Sounded like Marconi, I thought, looking at the painting on the wall that falsely portrayed him as youthful alongside his second wife.

"Now he's really yelling—" Jacob began. The bed curtains shifted.

Jacob flew back off his feet and slammed into the wall. It wasn't too far, and he landed on his feet, but it was definitely shocking.

Stacey shouted and ran to him, while I stepped toward the spot where he'd been, ready to blast my flashlight.

"Philip Marconi," I said, trying to act like I was in control, despite the fact that I so plainly wasn't. "Professor. Necromancer. You hoped and believed you summoned your wife Piper, but she was a fraud. An aufhocker pretended to be the ghost of Piper while it fed on you. Did you discover the truth, Dr. Marconi? Did the aufhocker murder you?"

The room grew even colder. In the shadows ahead I saw a figure that was tall and lean, much taller than the Gremel apparition had been. It was a featureless shadow at first. As it shifted toward me, floating rather than walking, its face came into view in the moonlight.

It was Marconi's face, or a version of it. I recognized the general appearance from his pictures, but this face was the color of stone, the eyes and mouth deep and dark like the features on an ancient Greek drama mask. He appeared to be wrapped in robes made of shadows.

"You know she tricked you," I guessed, drawing on one of our hypotheses. I tried to keep my voice level and not scream at the horrifying visage. My blood was like ice in the dead necromancer's presence. "Help us remove her from the house. Then you can move on—"

The figure vanished.

A second later, something hit me in the gut, painfully cold, with a lot of force.

I flew up and back until I slammed into the wall, high enough that my head thumped against the paneled ceiling.

Suddenly I felt dizzy and disoriented, just as I had up on the walkway. Maybe it was Marconi who'd tried to trick me into going the wrong way. Maybe he'd tried to kill me in the same spot where he'd died.

I filled the area with a flood from flashlight. Stacey and Jacob fired up their own, taking their cure from me. The room was suddenly blinding white.

Then Stacey added those ear-splitting church bells to the mix. The volume could have been a little lower, especially in that enclosed room.

I toppled to the floor, my eardrums more or less rupturing along the way. I landed roughly on my hands and knees. Stacey and Jacob ran to help me.

"I'm fine," I grumbled as they helped me up.

Marconi's ghost didn't grab me again right away; maybe he'd fled, or maybe he was still right beside me, watching and waiting.

"So, as I was saying, my delicate psychic senses

indicate this room might be haunted," Jacob said. "Regular people like you might not have noticed the little signs, like people being thrown around by invisible forces. But those of us who have the gift can pick up on subtleties like that."

"I think we're really upsetting him. Or it."

"That was my question," Stacey said. "Is it really *him*, or the, you know?" She glanced at Jacob, reminding me why she was being vague.

"The golf hacker?" Jacob said.

"You've heard of aufhocker*s*?" I asked.

"Yeah, just now, when you talked about it. You said it wasn't really his wife, it was a 'golf hacker' or something. I guess it hits the ball into the rough a lot."

I sighed. "We think it's a shapeshifting entity. So we're not sure whether that was really the person it looked like or just another illusion. It's been hard to identify which ghosts we might actually be dealing with, or even how many."

"We haven't seen this one before," Stacey added. "So, was that a new ghost or just a new face for the old one? That's the question."

"Let's let Jacob keep working," I said. "If he wants to."

"I was just here to help y'all figure out what's haunting this house. Then the ghost threw us against the wall." Jacob's voice dropped into a deep, serious, movie-advertisement-narrator tone. "And now it's personal. We won't stop until we have justice."

"Such a dork," Stacey whispered.

"Maybe we should keep moving," I suggested. I

was sure rougher times awaited us tonight.

Jacob nodded. He went on to check out the bathroom and the dance studio. "Look at that record player. It's like something from the Steam Age."

That was his only comment for that area. We continued down the hall, toward the second set of double doors, which would take us into the second story of the library. I'd left them open, but they were closed again.

I had more thoughts that I kept to myself for the moment. Like how the aufhocker usually took the form of dead loved ones, but none of us had loved Dr. Marconi, and researching the dead necromancer certainly hadn't led me to develop any kind of fondness for him. So I suspected we'd uncovered Marconi himself, not the aufhocker.

I couldn't be sure, though. There were still too many open questions about this case, and more of them opening up all the time.

We probably needed outside help on this one. Maybe James Lachlan, the former Jesuit, if he was available. Maybe there was someone more local.

I even considered the semi-wild Tucker Nealon, but he lived halfway across the country in Nacogdoches, Texas. Also, his last experience with us had left him burned, like physically burned by the worst pyrokinetic ghost I'd ever faced, so maybe he wouldn't care to take our calls.

The necromancer's library, and the quick translations Cherise had provided, had been a good source of information on the aufhocker, but I'd still found no way to banish the entity permanently. It was said to haunt empty roads, an undead thing feeding on those who traveled alone in the dark, the lost souls of the highway.

That got me exactly nowhere. It seemed to be an old demonic, though, and that likely meant bringing in an exorcist, if not the Texorcist.

"Whoa," Jacob said, stopping a few paces short of the closed doors. "That's a seriously decayed old guy standing there. He's pointing behind us. He wants us to leave. He's all bones and his clothes are like... I don't know... something from a Monty Python movie."

"A jerkin?" Stacey suggested.

"I guess. The jerk in the jerkin wants us to leave instead of going into the library."

"Don't mind him, he's just warning us it's dangerous in there," I said.

"Sounds like the place we need to be, then. Will something try to claw my face off the moment we open the doors?" Jacob asked.

"Possibly," I replied.

"Great." He took a deep breath, and together we pushed the heavy doors open.

Beyond, the library was as cold as a meat locker, as though it were filled with carcasses instead of rare books. The lights still didn't work here, and very little moonlight came in from the eastern windows. We'd clicked off our flashlights again.

Chaos lay all around us. Where the arches had collapsed, books lay strewn down the steep staircases, making them nearly impassable. Dense clumps of them blocked up some of the walkways.

The books that remained on the shelves were scrambled and overturned, splayed open to random pages.

Jacob leaned over the walkway railing to look down toward the first floor, which had become a somewhat post-apocalyptic book landfill.

"That's one messy library," Jacob whispered. "Is this the children's area or something?

"I don't think this library has a children's area," Stacey replied, also whispering. "The story time would give them nightmares."

Maybe it was the near total darkness of the place, but the library felt larger now than it had before. It was certainly colder.

"What's up there?" Jacob asked, as if something had caught his eye above us. He started toward it, and we knew where he was going right away.

"The railing's broken," Stacey warned, following close behind him. "You see the rope, right?"

"That rope is real?" Jacob said, acting over-the-top surprised. "I thought it was a *gho-o-st.*"

"Shut up. Just assume the whole railing is made of toothpicks, okay? It's not safe."

"Yet here we go, walking up there." Jacob cleared some books off a staircase so he could climb to the third floor. Stacey stuck right behind him, watching out for him like a mama bear with a really big cub.

The going was tougher than before. We had to clear books off the narrow walkways and push shelves back into place to clear the way forward.

"We should stay back, Jacob," Stacey whispered,

gripping his arm as he made his way, inevitably, toward the broken railing.

"Isn't that the window where we saw her earlier?" Jacob asked.

"It is," Stacey replied, sounding reluctant, as though not wanting to encourage him to investigate the area any longer.

"Something definitely happened here." Jacob walked up to the broken railing, which made Stacey cringe visibly. He closed his eyes, and his tone turned serious again. "Right here. He's looking down. His knee and hip ache from when he fell down in the yard a couple years ago, doing some basic shoveling. Old age, frailty, his body's getting useless. Death is with him every day like his shadow. He expects it at any moment, like a knock on the door, letting him know it's over.

"He envisions falling from here all the way, his body breaking on the floor like glass, or like a dead old tree that finally comes crashing down after years of rotting out. And if he dies here, he can stay here, in his library, in his house." Jacob's brow furrowed. "He's planning on dying and haunting the place. That's literally his plan. He's a real can of squirrels, this guy."

Can of squirrels? Stacey mouthed at me, but I could only shrug.

"He leans against the railing, and it cracks. Wait. There's someone beside him. An apparition. It's someone he lost. She's radiant. Beaming at him. She licks her lips like she's eager to watch it happen, to watch him die. She's pretty, really amazingly pretty to his eyes, he's like dazzled or hypnotized for this last moment because she's so—"

"Hey, watch out." Stacey elbowed Jacob back from the broken railing to keep him from the danger of falling, and maybe for other reasons.

"Then the railing breaks, and he falls. As he falls, he feels free. He hits the floor." Jacob stood for a long, quiet moment, still much too close to the railing, though Stacey kept a grip on him. "And he stays there, looking at his broken body. She's still there, his wife, clearer than ever. They become part of the house, and they wait."

"For what?" I asked. "What do they wait for, Jacob?"

"They... they..." Jacob opened his eyes. He gaped toward the window. In a different tone, he asked, "Ellie?"

"What, Jacob?"

"Does your research indicate a portal in this house? A gateway to the other side? Like the one that we found under Michael's apartment building?"

"Nope. Why?"

"I'm seeing someone I haven't seen..."

"Who are you seeing?"

"Jenny McAllister," he said, his voice a little awed. "She was my girlfriend in high school for a couple months."

"Eh, what?" Stacey asked, her forehead furrowing.

"Is she dead?" I asked. It was a little blunt, I probably should have phrased it more gently.

"Water skiing accident. She was sixteen. I was

supposed to be there, but I kind of hated her cousin who owned the boat, so I kind of backed out of going." He shook his head. "That guy was a jerk. I tried to convince her not to go. I should have tried harder."

"Whoa," Stacey said. "I did not know this."

"Now she's right there, dripping wet in her swimsuit. Her skin's blue. She's begging me to help her—"

"It's the aufhocker. She's trying to trick you."

"I don't know."

"Don't believe it, Jacob," I urged. "You have to fight back. You have to rebuke it. It's taken the form of one lost loved one after another."

"Including your dead girlfriend," Stacey said, sounding somewhat annoyed. "Which I am sorry to hear about. But this isn't her. She's gone. Like Ellie says—rebuke it. Somehow."

"You're not Jenny," Jacob finally said, taking our advice, though his tone was a bit reluctant. "Show me your true face, demon. Show your face and give your name."

A throaty growling sounded.

A dark, shaggy shape slouched before the window, blocking the moonlight. Lurking in the shadows of the unlit library, it was neither wolf nor bear but could have resembled either at a distance, a nightmarish blend of the great predators that hunted our prehistoric ancestors.

Stacey and I struck with the church bells in stereo.

The thing snarled and turned to a swirling black

fog as it left the walkway, shattering the rest of the damaged railing into splinters. Broken balusters rained down to the snowdrift of broken books on the first story far below.

The railing across the way shattered, and the thick pile of fallen books behind it spilled to the library floor like water from behind a ruptured dam.

The spindly walkway support columns cracked, and the entire second-story walkway across from us swung down like it was on a hinge. It dumped out all its fallen books at once.

Similar cracking sounds erupted right below us.

"Run!" I shouted, as we all took off, racing to escape the walkway before it could collapse beneath us.

The next intersection was too distant, though. Our walkway dropped away before we could reach it.

We scrambled to grab onto the bookshelves in front of us. Some of these random wild grabs turned out to be luckier than others.

The shelf I grabbed with my left hand turned out to be quite loose, and it slid out of my grasp, along with the overturned books it held. This was not a great outcome.

I ended up swinging the shelf out into the empty space behind me. The books slid off, and I finally had the presence of mind to release the useless shelf. It fell after the books and cracked loudly when it struck a tabletop below, giving me a taste of what might happen to my backbone should I fall.

Fortunately, my right hand had managed to grab a hard dividing wall between bookshelves. It wasn't sliding anywhere, but it was vertical and narrow, so my grasp was dangerously awkward and slippery.

The toe of my left boot had landed atop a row of leather-bound volumes, but there was no telling how strong the bookshelf beneath it was or how long it might support my weight before collapsing, perhaps with some help from the aufhocker who'd apparently had enough of us.

Farther along, the moonlit shapes of Stacey and Jacob also held onto bookshelves as best they could. Neither had fallen yet, luckily. Like me, they clung there desperately like monkeys on a wall, or like the incredibly cheesy old-time black and white serials Jacob liked to watch, where the hero would inevitably be left hanging on the edge of a cliff; in the old days, the movie audience would have to wait until the following week to see whether the hero survived the next chapter.

Chapter Twenty-Two

The aufhocker remained invisible, or at least out of sight, but we could hear its low growl, and feel the shuddering and shaking as it tore apart the rickety network of walkways and staircases on the second and third level.

"Let's move!" I shouted to Stacey. "But carefully," I added.

"Oh, this is just like free bouldering," Stacey said. "Which I don't like. Give me a harness if I'm going up steep rocks, you know? I don't want to bash my brains out—"

"More moving, less explaining," I suggested.

We climbed sideways across the bookshelves— me, then Jacob, then Stacey. Some of the shelves broke under my weight, but some didn't. It was a game of Russian roulette as we slowly approached the next walkway, which itself was badly sloped, some of its supports broken.

Once there, we hurried to the next staircase, only to find it smashed to bits. We continued onward toward the next one.

Something cold and hard, and unfortunately familiar, hit me just below the rib cage, slamming me back into Jacob and Stacey.

We sprawled together in a tangle on a walkway that was as springy as a rope bridge but really shouldn't have been.

The tall shape loomed over us, gray Greek mask of a bearded face, eyes sunken deep, a cloak of darkness shrouding his body. The necromancer.

I gestured for Stacey to turn off her church bells. They weren't keeping the necromancer away, and my head was pounding from them.

"Philip Marconi," I said. "You were deceived. Gremel's book is a fraud. You did not draw Piper down from paradise, but summoned a dangerous and deceptive spirit into your home. You must feel it by now, especially as a spirit, that she who shares your home is not truly... uh, hello? Dr. Phil?"

Marconi drifted through the air, past me and Jacob, and now seemed to orbit Stacey slowly, his deep eye sockets fixated on her. The hints of actual eyes seemed to glimmer within the depths, for the first time, gray lights in deep caverns.

"Why is he doing that?" Stacey whispered through a wide, fake, toothy smile. "What did I do?"

"I don't think it's anything you did." I drew a small object from my jeans pocket, then took Stacey's hand. I slid it onto her ring finger.

"Uh, Ellie?" Stacey held up the diamond wedding ring. "I mean, first off, this is really a complete surprise—"

"Shut up. You kind of look like Piper."

"I do? Thanks."

"Yeah, blonde hair, similar build. Now look at him."

Marconi drew closer to her. The eyes within his sunken sockets seemed clearer now, dilated black pupils, irises as stone gray as his face.

"Great. He likes me," Stacey said, without a glint of happiness in her tone.

"Send him after the aufhocker," I said.

"Okay. Marconi, go attack the aufhocker! Like, now, please."

Marconi drew back a little. It was hard to read his stone mask face.

Then another support must have gone out, because our walkway lurched hard and sloped sharply to one side.

"Help us!" Stacey screamed, and the thing drew back further and vanished.

"Good enough for me," Jacob said.

We got moving, struggling for balance on the tilted and wobbling walkway, then clambering down a loose staircase cluttered with books that made us trip and stumble at every step. We reached a second-story walkway, which immediately collapsed.

We dropped a full story through empty space

and landed hard atop the fallen avalanche of books. Hardcovers. Paperbacks would have been better. I really would have preferred a periodical section with nice, soft newspapers and magazines.

"Groan," Stacey finally said. "My ribs. I got rib-poked by some kind of Encyclopedia Occultica."

We got to our feet and walked as best as we could, the poor old books forming a shifting, quicksand-like surface as we trudged over them.

"Jacob, any idea where they went?" I asked.

"They haven't left." Jacob turned and pointed at a relatively undisturbed section of bookshelves built into the wall. "They're standing there. The old guy and the blonde girl. Watching us."

"Why there?" It seemed like a fairly random section of bookshelves, a reference area full of old dictionaries, encyclopedias, and atlases, all in suspiciously good order compared to the rest of the room.

"I'm not sure," Jacob said. "They look furious, though."

I drew on my thermal goggles.

Through them, I saw the cold spots where the entities stood, one a deep blue, the other a tumorous purple-black, extra large and extra cold. I guessed the bigger, darker, colder one was the aufhocker.

My goggles also picked up thin blue lines in the bookshelves behind the two cold spots, like drafts leaking through. These were perfectly straight, a rectangular outline in the shape of a wide door.

"There's something behind those bookshelves." I started toward them, even as Jacob yelled for me to wait.

And then everything started toward us.

It wasn't just books. Some of the more cutting-edge contents of the Tomb Room had been moved out here—blades, swords, heavy candlesticks, bones sharpened and painted with occult symbols, assorted skulls, some animal, some that might have been human. We certainly hadn't seen those before. Maybe they'd come from monkeys or other primates; I didn't have much of a chance to inspect them.

The books and artifacts hammered us from all sides as if flung by tornado-force winds. The heavy Anubis statue slammed into me like an attack dog, the death god's silver jackal teeth biting into my shoulder. I grabbed the statue with both hands and flung it to the floor.

"This way!" I continued charging directly toward the bookshelves, through the hurricane of heavy books and artifacts that struck and stabbed at us.

When I reached the shelves, I shoved the books off as fast as I could, pushing them carelessly onto the floor as I searched for whatever latch or mechanism would open the bookcase and reveal the hidden space beyond. Jacob and Stacey did the same.

Something grabbed me from behind, lifted me off my feet, and carried me upward at a frightening speed.

I barely had time to realize what was happening before I slammed into the pressed-tin ceiling. Then I hung there, suspended. It felt like a freezing cold hand was pushing against my chest, pinning me there like a captured bug. The air was thick and foul, hard to breathe.

The unseen force made it difficult for me to reach the defensive tools on my belt.

"What are you doing with her?" The woman's voice almost boiled over with rage, which was why it took me a moment to realize it was actually the normally very chill Stacey. She stood amid the scattered books and pointed up at me, the enormous diamond of Piper's wedding ring glinting on her finger. "Philip, get your hands off that girl!"

This proved a clever move. Maybe too clever, because I immediately plummeted through the thick, freezing cold space. I barely had time to position my fall so I'd bruise my hip instead of breaking my neck.

I slammed hard into a pile of books. It wasn't quite freefall speed; falling straight through the entity that had captured me had slowed me a little bit. Not enough to stop the impact from lashing my entire side with pain.

Jacob hurried to help me up, while Stacey continued pointing an accusing finger at the space above me.

"You okay?" Jacob asked.

"I'm about ready to check out of this library," I muttered, drawing my flashlight but keeping it off.

Stacey jumped back against Jacob.

Marconi's apparition had materialized close to her, his colorless eyes staring from the sunken depths of his stony gray face. He reached a dead-gray hand toward Stacey, and she cringed.

Another apparition appeared nearby, not far from me. While the necromancer's apparition was faint and colorless, the new one was strong and clear, a pale blonde girl, her eyes and her silky dress ice blue. It looked like Piper, but had to be the aufhocker wearing her form.

Marconi hesitated and looked back at her.

"Philip!" Stacey snapped, sounding furious. The art school graduate was really in character. "Leave her alone. She's false. She's not me."

The Piper apparition looked as angry as Stacey sounded. She reached a hand toward Marconi's apparition, as if summoning him.

An eyeblink later, Marconi stood beside the Piper apparition, at her side like an obedient dog.

"No!" Stacey snapped. "She's deceiving you!"

"Show your true form, golf hacker," Jacob said in a commanding tone.

"Aufhocker," I corrected without looking. I was already back at the bookshelf, once again trying to find the way through.

I knocked a row of books off one shelf, but one volume refused to budge, even when I pulled hard on it. *The Doors of Perception* by Aldous Huxley.

I pushed it instead. This brought a soft, satisfying click.

A doorway-sized section of shelves swung inward, revealing narrow stairs that led down and twisted out of sight.

"There's more to the cellar," Jacob said, his gaze following my light. "I knew it."

Piper's apparition dropped its jaw and let out a

long screeching scream, like she was a banshee instead of an aufhocker. Marconi rushed toward us.

"This way!" I shouted, then bolted down the stairs, with no time to look where I was going.

We arrived in a space resembling the other cellar, with dusty brick columns supporting the house above. The shelves here contained books instead of strange jars of long-forgotten slime preserves.

The entities didn't pursue us immediately. I shone my light around the irregular, shadowy space, while Jacob stood with his eyes closed, trying to pick up any subtle signals, any paranormal secrets hiding in the dark.

"Oh, sick!" Stacey announced. She'd opened a random book from the shelves, and now looked ill, as if she'd taken a deep sniff of a jug full of chunky sour milk. She slammed the cover and returned the book.

"What was that?" I asked.

"Looked like some kind of perverse, gross magical rituals. Graphically illustrated. With bodily fluids everywhere. *All* the bodily fluids, I think—"

"She's here," Jacob said, interrupting Stacey, for which I was grateful.

"Who?" I asked.

"Nirvana Girl."

As he said it, my flashlight found a disturbing tableau near the back of the room: a cot, a small plastic cooler like you might take camping if you're into that, and a steel chain with handcuffs. The chain was padlocked to one of the house's brick supports.

"I thought Nirvana Girl wouldn't come inside

the house," I said to Jacob while trying to process what I saw.

"Under the house is different," Jacob said. "She's connected to this room. She was kept here. Imprisoned. Night after night, something came for her in the dark. Something that tried to invade her. Possess her. It had the face of a dead woman, shriveled and wrinkled, the teeth crooked and sharp, the eyes full of evil."

I pictured the aufhocker statue from Germany, the hooded goblin-like creature perched on the back of its victim, its face similar to what Jacob was describing.

A table near the cot held empty water bottles and a couple of empty, crumpled potato chip bags. I opened the table drawer.

"Hey," I said, holding a thin stack of hand-written pages held together by a clamp. They were raggedly torn along one edge, as if they'd been ripped out of something. "I think we found the missing pages of Marconi's journal."

"They tried, but it didn't work..." Jacob winced, his eyes still closed. "She resisted. She fought. She prayed. The entity didn't succeed in possessing her, and it all started to drag on too long. One day Marconi came down with a knife instead of food and water. The old man stabbed her and stabbed her —"

"That's awful!" Stacey shouted.

"—he made a sacrifice of her. Sacrificed her to the spirit of his dead wife, who became stronger as a result. She helped give the old man the strength to wrap her body, drag it to his car, and bury it in the cemetery out back." He opened his eyes. "Ellie, behind you."

I turned, facing the freezing air.

Apparitions of Marconi and Piper stood there, and though I'd expected to see them, I still gasped, my pulse kicking up as I expected another attack. No trace of Marconi's colorless eyes remained in his deep, dark sockets, just empty darkness.

Piper's apparition glowed coldly, her face staring at me with pure hate.

"Uh-oh," Jacob said. "They're really furious now —"

The psychokinetic attack ripped through the room like freezing tornado winds. The cot and table were overturned, and the three of us were knocked from our feet.

Something slammed above us, in the direction of the stairs.

"Did we just get locked in?" Stacey gasped.

I turned my light toward the two apparitions, but they'd vanished.

"Let's go!" I shouted, darting up the stairs. The hidden bookcase door had indeed closed, sealing us in, and showed no sign of budging. It was latched, and the latch wouldn't move.

"They want to kill us," Jacob said. His voice was deadpan, all his usual humor gone.

I hammered my flashlight into the wood next to the latch. After the third blow, I heard a pleasant cracking sound.

We shoved the hidden door open and staggered

out into the library.

Unfortunately, this meant the two angry spirits had plenty of ammunition. Books and artifacts slammed into us from every side.

Over near the concealed, closed door to the Tomb Room, Gremel had appeared just as I'd seen him on our first night here, his body a rotten skeleton, his jerkin grungy and decayed.

"Help us!" I shouted at him.

Gremel pointed one bony finger at the bookshelves behind him. That was apparently the best he could do, standing and pointing.

I bolted toward him, taking heavy blows to my arms as I threw them up to cover my face. More books pelted my back, some of them bursting into clouds of old paper on impact. Something stabbed into my leg. I didn't have time to investigate. It was all I could do to avoid tripping and falling over the countless shifting obstacles underfoot.

The Tomb Room's roll-aside door was closed and locked, despite the fact that many of its more obviously dangerous contents were already out in the main library being flung against us.

I fumbled through the key ring while more books pelted me. My leg was bleeding from a splinter of hard leather book binding that had stabbed me there.

Stacey and Jacob were nearly lost in the gloom and chaos. Their flashlight beams swung erratically as they knocked away flying debris, illuminating little more than glimpses of the madness around us.

Finally, I rolled the door open and lurched

inside.

The Tomb Room had never been well organized, but at this point it was in less disarray than most of the library outside, as though the destructive spirits valued the books in this room more highly than the rest.

"Gremel?" I shone my flashlight, but he didn't materialize. Of course, the full-spectrum white light was not ghost friendly, so I snuffed it out and lit one of the many candles using one of the late professor's wooden matches.

There, in the flickering candlelight, Gremel materialized, again pointing with his bony finger, toward the desk nearby.

Toward his own book.

"Yeah, I'm not falling for that," I said. "Marconi tried your spell for bringing back the dead. All it brought him was the aufhocker. Give me a reason to trust you."

Gremel hesitated, thinking, maybe. It's hard to read the expression of a thing that's only a shadowy, candle-lit apparition, especially when that thing's face has mostly rotted away.

Then he pointed toward the ritual objects we'd pulled out of the candle-wax table.

I looked, not eager to touch any of it, and saw him reflected in the black crystal scrying ball, his features a little clearer there, though no less rotten.

In the reflection, glinting metallic links floated in the space between his neck and his reptile-hide book.

"You're chained to the book?" I asked.

He quickly raised his rotten, pointing hand toward my face, which was a little horrifying, but which I also took as a yes. If he'd known how to play charades, he might have tapped his nose hole to show I was figuring things out.

"Ah. So you wear the chain you forged in life, like Jacob Marley?"

He didn't respond. Probably much too old to understand a Charles Dickens reference.

"Is that your punishment for creating the book?" I clarified. I pointed to the book, and so did he. "The book is evil. It's a trap for those who use it. Like Marconi."

If he responded, it was probably in German on an auditory frequency I couldn't detect without enhancement. As it was, he went back to our usual method of communication, him pointing and freezing while I did the rest.

I'd assumed he was telling me to follow his own banishment spell for the summoned souls, and maybe he was, but I trusted that about as much as I trusted my cat around a tuna sandwich while I was out of the room. It obviously hadn't gone right for Marconi, who'd summoned a shapeshifting demonic entity when he'd wanted his wife.

Regardless of what he meant, he was pointing to the page that had the illustration of a dagger and a cup, which got me thinking. I looked at the implements on the table, recalled Marconi's journal, and nodded.

There are methods that I prefer to avoid in this work, paths I prefer not to walk. I like the ghost traps because they're distant, clinical, technological. And I like it when spirits move on, or get forced to, because that's convenient.

What I truly hate is the kind of thing I was about to do next.

I picked up the golden goblet and the ivory, golden blade with the golden hilt.

The pale blonde Piper apparition stood before me almost instantly.

I touched the tip of the blade to the skin of my wrist.

The beautiful apparition licked her lips as a drop of blood welled up on my flesh.

Out in the library, silence had fallen. I heard Jacob and Stacey speaking to each other, but couldn't make out their words.

I looked at the crystal ball again. In its reflection, the Marconi apparition was faintly visible, standing in the room with us. Watching.

"You want a sacrifice, aufhocker?" I asked, since I had no real name for the entity, only its type. "Come with me."

Carrying the blade and cup, I returned to the main library.

"Ellie, what's happening?" Stacey asked. They both looked battered but definitely alive.

"I'm trying something. Come on. Everyone follow me." I meant that message for all of them, the living and the dead.

We pushed our way out through the first-floor dark doors. Despite my injuries, I only stopped a moment, long enough to draw the long sliver of dried leather book cover from my leg. Stacey wanted to stop and bandage me, but I brushed her off. "Not until it's over," I whispered.

I limped up the front stairs, leaving droplets of blood. Maybe they would whet the aufhocker's appetite, keep it hot on my trail. Jacob and Stacey helped me drag the big stamper from Cherise's room to the master suite, into Marconi's old bedroom.

I'd already removed our previous bait, the wedding rings. Now I placed the small gold chalice at the bottom of the trap, and again touched the bloodied tip of the ivory blade to the broken skin on my wrist.

The aufhocker appeared right away, still wearing Piper's form.

I was pretty sure that if I dripped a little blood into the goblet, she'd focus herself down on that sacrifice, that primitive offering of flesh to spirit, long enough for me to snap the trap shut.

But I wanted one more thing from her first.

"Show me my father again," I said.

The Piper apparition looked at me with her pale blue eyes.

"My father. If you want anything from me, let me speak to him again."

She smiled. Smirked almost. Then she was gone.

"Eleanor." My father's ghost stepped out from the shadows of the old wardrobe, like he was just dropping by from Narnia. He was smiling, relaxed, wearing a blue work shirt and jeans. "It's good to see you."

"You, too, Dad. I want to give you something." I

held out my pierced wrist and squeezed, making the blood well up. "That will make you strong again. That will bring you back. Won't it, Daddy?"

"Yes." He stared transfixed at the blood and licked his lips. "Yes, it will, Pumpkin."

Shivering, trying not to cry, I turned my arm and let the blood drip into the golden chalice down at the bottom of the trap. "My offering," I whispered.

My father vanished. It had never really been him, but it still hurt, strangely, to see the illusion go.

I reached out to close the trap, but the aufhocker's presence triggered the temperature and electromagnetic sensors before I even touched the control. The trap closed automatically, the lid slamming shut.

Inside, a black fog filled the innermost leaded-glass layer of the trap.

I looked toward the bed curtains. "Did you see?"

The curtains shifted.

Marconi appeared in the shadows, barely visible.

"Did you see?" I repeated. "It was not Piper. It never was. It was an illusion."

I gestured at Stacey without looking away from Marconi's apparition. I had to force the aufhocker to shapeshift in Marconi's presence so he would see the entity's true nature.

I had no idea how he might react to this news, but a violent lashing out seemed possible.

Stacey picked up on my gesturing and unloaded the trap from the stamper. The strange, oily-black cloud inside it momentarily formed a suggestion of a scowling, hooded, goblin-like face glaring out at her.

She grimaced and set it down quickly, and the fog within vanished from sight, the entity either choosing to go invisible or possessing too little energy to keep up an apparition.

Stacey replaced the first trap with a spare stored on the stamper's side.

Marconi advanced on Stacey, his interest in her possibly rekindled by the discovery that the aufhocker was a fraud. The guy was desperate to see Piper one way or another.

"Take off the ring, Stacey," I told her, holding out my hand.

"Does this mean we're not engaged anymore, Ellie?" She pouted as she gave the diamond ring back. "It all happened so fast."

I drew Dr. Marconi's ring from my pocket and held both wedding rings out toward the ghost, who drew close to them.

"You could move on," I said. "Let go of this world. Move on up, or down, or wherever you're supposed to go."

He kept his sunken eyes fixed on the rings.

"But you kidnapped and murdered that girl. So as far as I'm concerned..." I dropped both rings into the ghost trap. "In you go."

Marconi vanished, and the stamper slammed down again, sealing him inside.

"Wow," Stacey said, after a long moment. "We actually trapped a ghost. I mean, how often does that actually happen?"

"We trapped two, even," I said. "Marked for toxic disposal, I'd say."

"Reverend Mordecai's old mountain boneyard for the evil dead?" Stacey asked.

"Sounds right to me. Jacob, want to go on a hike? Stacey's probably lulled you into enjoying that kind of thing."

"She almost has, yeah," Jacob said. "Nature has terrible WiFi, though."

"Let me see your leg." Stacey drew a small first aid kit from her backpack and looked over my leg. "I guess I'll have to cancel our bridal registry."

"I already have a gravy boat, anyway," I said.

"I really wanted that crystal candy dish. You know, for guests."

"I'm pretty confused," Jacob said. "Just tell me whether there's a third ghost who's going to come charging out trying to kill us, or if that was it."

"There's a third ghost," I said. "He was pretty evil in life, I think, but he has his own reasons for helping us."

I explained about Gremel, what I knew as well as what I suspected about why he'd been helping us, as we returned to the library.

We stood at the entrance to the library, shining our lights around the destruction. Fallen bookshelves, collapsed walkways, shattered staircases and heaps and heaps of destroyed books. Broken skulls. The death god Anubis lay cracked on his side, his silver teeth chipped.

"Bad god," I whispered to the canine form of Anubis as I passed him. My shoulder still ached from

when he'd bashed into me; good thing I'd been
wearing my leather jacket to protect against his bite.
"That's a bad, bad god."

We headed into the Tomb Room. I propped the
door open with a chair again, just to be safe. It was
extremely cold inside.

"He's here," Jacob said in a low voice as I joined
him and Stacey.

"At least the grim reaper painting didn't get
hurt," Stacey noticed, looking at the skull-faced soul
collectors in their field of dead flowers. "You think
that would look good in my apartment?"

"Are you seeing Gremel?" I asked Jacob.

"He's wearing an iron collar and chain," Jacob
said. "I mean, they're psychological, you know, not
really iron, but they feel like iron. He's chained to
this... this reptile book. Who made this? Salazar
Slytherin?" He grimaced as he moved the dried
snake-tail bookmark aside.

"Gremel made it," I told him.

"Ooh, Jacob's a Ravenclaw," Stacey said.

"Gryffindor," he said absently. "Though I could
have done well in Slytherin. But it looks like Gremel
walked on the Slytherin side. This is some dark,
twisted..." Jacob paused, looking from the picture of
the dagger and chalice to the wound I'd stabbed into
my arm. "You've got that thing solidly trapped,
right?"

"Right," I said. "Why?"

"You made a blood sacrifice to it."

I felt my blood run cold, though not from any
of my recent wounds. "Yeah. I mean, kind of. As a

trick. Why, uh, are you bringing up that definitely small and unimportant detail?"

"It could create a bond between you and it."

"Ew," Stacey said. "Ellie's bonding with and marrying people left and right tonight. I feel less special now. Our engagement is definitely off."

"What kind of bond?" I asked Jacob.

"I'm not sure. Just bury that trap deep."

"So that's settled," I insisted with a nod. "What about Gremel? Can we help him?"

"Help him?" Jacob looked confused.

"He's been helping us," Stacey said. "Maybe we should help him move on from his eternal curse if we can. It's the polite thing."

"Every time the book is used, that's another link in the chain," Jacob said. "The more suffering his book causes, the more he endures, and the longer his curse grows. Maybe each length of the chain lengthens the amount of time of he has to spend trapped on the Earth, or makes his existence more miserable."

"And that's why he's been helping us," I said. "The less damage done as a result of the book, the less punishment inflicted on him."

"And here I just thought he was a nice old rotten ghost in a jerkin," Stacey said.

"He wasn't being altruistic. It was just self-interested damage control," I said. "Trying to keep himself in the higher circles of Hell and out of the lower ones, I guess. Would destroying the book help him?"

Jacob nodded. "But if there's no book, it can't

cause any more pain, and his chain can't grow any longer. Am I right? So it feels weird to say it, but in this case we might think about a small book burning. Just this one book. Okay, he's pointing his bony finger right at my face—"

"That means he thinks you're onto something," I said. "Sounds like he likes you."

"Great. Well, let's burn it somewhere outside, because evil spellbook dead-reptile fumes can't be healthy. Also, once the sun's up, somebody needs to open all those windows." He pointed up at the walled-off area around us, creating the three-story Tomb Room with all its heavy dark shelves. "This place still crawls with little entities, slumbering, and some of them might be dangerous. These books and artifacts are dangerous. Something has to be done with them."

"We have a very large safe for this kind of material in the basement back at the office," I said. "Can you help us identify what needs to be quarantined?"

Jacob nodded. "Bear in mind, I have to be back at work Monday morning."

"We have time. Our client's on track to inherit the place. All she has to do is take care of the library."

"Could be problems with that," Stacey said.

We walked out into the mounds of destroyed books, the snowdrift of loose and torn pages. Knowledge, history, stories, myths, and poetry lay hopelessly mixed, the thoughts and ideas of thousands of years mingled together in a great babble of confusion.

Chapter Twenty-Three

"These are the missing pages from Marconi's journal," I said, spreading them out on the kitchen table in front of Cherise, amid sunlight and coffee cups. "They're pretty disturbing."

"That's nothing new at this point," Cherise said. She took a long sip of coffee. On my advice, she'd left her younger sister with a friend in Athens for the day. Too many concerns remained about both the structural and spiritual integrity of the house, and I also wanted to give Cherise the chance to filter what Aria heard about all this. Stacey sat with us. Jacob dozed upstairs in our borrowed bedroom.

"We learned he kidnapped a college student for the aufhocker to possess—for his wife's spirit to

possess, he thought—but the student resisted too
well, and eventually they murdered her," I said.
There was no easy way to say it.

Cherise winced. "Here in the house?"

"Yes. Down in the hidden room below the
library. And they buried her in the cemetery out
back. It was her voice we recorded out there, asking
for help."

"That's awful."

"Since that possession failed, they made a new
plan: you. He told Dr. Anderson he preferred
someone female. And someone 'deserving' who was
in financial need."

"She was going to possess me?" Cherise asked.

"That's why he wanted someone full-time here.
Someone they could constantly work on and
gradually take over, with a timeframe of weeks and
months instead of days—this period of weakening
the living is called oppression, and it lays the
groundwork for actual possession. But then they
found out about your sister."

"I brought her with me a couple of times,"
Cherise said quietly, a look of guilt on her face. "She
was supposed to help me. Ended up sitting around
with her headphones and tablet the whole time."

"The aufhocker wanted to possess your sister
instead. So that led to the new plan—Marconi would
die and leave you the house."

"Dr. Marconi actually planned to die?" Cherise
asked.

"And then come back. By possessing your body,
while the aufhocker—who he believed to be his wife

—possessed your sister's."

"His plan was for him and his dead wife to take over a pair of sisters? That's... bizarre. And sick. In so many ways," Cherise said. She had the flat affect of someone repeatedly hit by shocking information until she couldn't do much more than take mental notes for later.

"True. He wrote it would deepen their connection to be siblings instead of married partners. He said it would be a 'profound reincarnational relationship' in the journal. In other places he called it 'soul play.' Kind of like 'role play' but—"

"I'll read it for myself. Sometime. Maybe." Cherise glanced at the journal pages like they were dead rats on her kitchen table. "At least things fit together now. He gave me his whole estate because it wasn't going to be *me* living my life. It was going to be him, wearing my body like Buffalo Bill from *Silence of the Lambs.*"

"Well, yes. He was basically giving it all to himself. Once they fully possessed you and Aria, they'd have decades of life ahead. He didn't want to leave all his wealth behind. You know what they say about money and material things, that you can't take it with you? He wanted to take it with him, into his next life."

"As me." Cherise shook her head. "I never liked that old man, honestly. You're not supposed to speak ill of the dead, or of your employer, at least where it might get back to him, so I haven't said much, but he always made me uncomfortable. I wanted to believe he was this frail, harmless elderly man who loved books, but his eyes... he had the most evil look, especially when he was watching me and he thought I didn't know it. I started to think he was undressing me with his eyes. Turns out he was thinking about my body in even worse ways than that." She shivered. "I don't know if I can come back here. I definitely can't live here anymore."

"I wouldn't recommend it until we can get all those windows open, maybe burn some sage, and get the house blessed by your preferred religious leader. And clear the occult stuff out of the Tomb Room. We have a place to store things like that. As for the rest of the collection, I could put in a call to Grant Patterson at the Savannah Historical Association. He can probably put together some people to help you reorganize and salvage what's left of the library. Maybe even repair some of the books."

"But you probably want to look at repairing the house, too," Stacey said.

"I'll call Marconi's lawyer tomorrow," Cherise said. "He's the executor, so he's the only one who can pay for all that. All I have is the stipend. Then it's over. Obviously I can't finish this project. Too much was destroyed, and I can't continue here. I won't inherit the house, but who wants it, anyway?"

"Nobody in their right mind," Stacey said. "But, hey, that still leaves Vic Marconi. He'll take it if you don't want it."

"If I don't complete the job, the estate will be broken up and donated. He still doesn't get the house."

"That brings us to something else we found in the hidden room." I handed over a thick three-ring binder.

Cherise opened it. Her brow furrowed. It furrowed deeper and deeper as she turned the pages. "This is a catalog of Marconi's collection. I was supposed to spend a year compiling this."

"That was just busy work to keep you spending long hours in the haunted library," I said. "He figured he would have you completely possessed in a matter of months. Once he had control of you, he'd go down to the hidden room, retrieve this, and present it to the lawyer. As you, he would then become the full owner of the entire estate. There's a CD copy in the back flap."

Cherise looked between me and Stacey and the book a few times. I doubt she was having trouble understanding me, but the implications for her were enormous.

"So, I turn this in," she said. "And then I get it all. I could do it tomorrow."

"Exactly," I said. "All of his personal and investment properties become yours."

Cherise continued staring at the binder, her mouth open.

"In light of this information, we'll probably charge you like crazy for this investigation," I said. "If that's okay."

"Oh, sure," Cherise said, still thumbing through pages. "Yeah. Easy come, easy go. You've earned it."

"You'll barely notice the dent in your fortune, I

promise."

Cherise just stared at the binder. "Okay. Wow. Thanks."

"We'll get started packing up our gear." I nodded to Stacey, and we both stood up. We had plenty of work ahead, squaring away all the threads of this case.

We left Cherise there in the kitchen, quietly looking over the binder and the journal pages, processing all we'd told her—the good, the bad, the unexpected.

Outside, in the small fire pit Stacey had dug in the back yard, the last ashes of Gremel's book lay cool and gray, and a light rain began to fall through the sunlit morning.

I didn't know whether Gremel's soul was free— the man had clearly done his share of evil in life— but at least his book wouldn't cause any more suffering, and the chain on his soul would grow no longer.

Chapter Twenty-Four

The office of Eckhart Investigations is not in a pretty building, nor in a pretty part of town—our neighbor is an auto salvage yard—but for some purposes, it's really the best place. For one thing, the rent is cheap, and Calvin has an apartment on the top floor, though he primarily lives in Florida now.

The basement holds an eight-foot, lead-lined steel safe that's best kept isolated from civilization. It's meant to hold dangerous artifacts, to quarantine them from the world.

Calvin was in town, watching from his wheelchair as Stacey and I finished loading the worst bits of the necromancer's library onto the shelves within the safe.

We'd quarantined the ritual dagger, plus assorted books and other items Jacob had identified as harboring particularly negative energy, and also the statue of Anubis. Jacob said it really wasn't all that cursed, but I didn't trust it. I wanted that death god idol kept in the pound.

"It's quite the shocking story," Calvin said, looking up from the *Athens Banner-Herald* he was reading. "Ridley Lovett, a student missing for three years. Found murdered by a professor and buried in his yard. They've exhumed her from the cemetery now and returned her remains to her family. Hopefully that will give her peace. It's certainly not justice. The poor girl, kidnapped and stabbed to death because an old man couldn't accept the natural order of things. Not like me. I've already got my grave picked out."

"You've got plenty of years left, Calvin," I said.

"How are you holding up after such a rough case?" Calvin asked, looking from me to Stacey. He'd originally hired her to assist me as he'd eased back from working the cases himself. "It sounds psychologically demanding. This entity made it personal for everyone."

"We're great," Stacey said. "We don't fear the dead. The dead fear us. Right, Ellie?"

"Right." I watched Stacey depart through the door to the concrete stairwell beyond.

"She's working out fine, isn't she?" Calvin asked.

"Is that an apologetic tone I'm detecting?" I asked. "Yes, she's fine."

"I'm sorry I wasn't there for you on a case this

dangerous."

"Nah, I can handle an old bookworm and his demon girlfriend. It's the books I feel bad for. Anyway, I had a dead German wizard helping me. One tiny little blood sacrifice into the aufhocker's favorite goblet, and boom, she was in the trap. I mean *it*. It wasn't necessarily a female spirit."

"What blood?" Calvin's eyes widened and went to my bandaged arm.

I shrugged. "I was the handiest source. Jacob said later it was a bad idea, that maybe I'd bonded with the aufhocker like a divorced dad taking his kids to Legoland."

"If it escapes, it might come looking for you," Calvin said.

"Well, I can name a long list of entities who'd like to come after me for some revenge. These two will be buried alongside some of them." I gestured at the two ghost traps on the rack in the corner, one holding the necromancer's soul and two wedding rings, the other holding the aufhocker and the golden chalice stained with my blood. We had stored these down here, keeping them far away from the empty traps in the storage room and van upstairs. "Let's hope they don't all get together and start a band. The Ungrateful Dead."

"Bury them deep."

"That's just what Jacob said."

"A little of your essence might be going down with them."

"Not reassuring, but I'll try my best to forget it. Anything else?"

"One more question. Chinese or pizza?"

"Pizza," I said. "After the week we had? Definitely pizza."

I busied myself with the task of picking and ordering pizza for the three of us. It was the most pleasant thing I'd done all week.

Chapter Twenty-Five

I wasn't looking forward to the hike to Reverend Mordecai's graveyard—I never do—but Stacey decided it could be turned into a fun event with boyfriends and picnic baskets. I agreed to it, provided we didn't picnic anywhere near the old burial ground itself. Apparently people used to picnic in cemeteries in the nineteenth century, but it's definitely not for me. Even if it was, I would never pick that particular cemetery.

So, a couple of weeks after winding down the case, we found ourselves spending a Sunday afternoon high up in the northwest corner of our state, in an area where the rough, steep land kept human settlement sparse.

It was March, which can mean winter or spring in Georgia, but it was definitely chilly at the high elevation we'd reached. I hadn't dressed thickly, knowing I'd be sweating bullets on the long, steep hike along an overgrown trail that barely existed outside the imagination of local rabbits and deer.

Indeed, I was damp with sweat. Michael walked beside me in a long-sleeved white t-shirt, looking like he was enjoying a downhill stroll on a cool day. He carried a shovel but didn't even bother using it as a walking stick, which he totally could have. I guess the firefighter training prepared him for extreme situations like this. He also seemed to enjoy going to the gym. Weirdo.

Stacey was on top of things, too, but Jacob was panting. Accountant training is very different than firefighter training. Maybe he and I needed to start a support group.

"Are we there yet?" I asked, though I was the one leading the way.

"When we see the two-inch thorns and the poison oak and poison ivy everywhere, then we'll know we've reached the edge of Reverend Blake's Churchyard of Terror," Stacey said.

"What's the story with this place, exactly?" Michael asked. "Why do you bury them here?"

"There once was a real fire-breathing mountain preacher named Mordecai Blake who went off the crazy-cult rails and took the whole tiny isolated community with him," Stacey said, not huffing or puffing at all as we trudged upward through dense brambles. "Tell them about the Sinner's Box."

"It was the Judgment Box," I said. "If you sinned, or angered Blake—if you tried to run away, or just looked at him wrong—he'd lock you into this wooden box for judgment. You'd be trapped in the dark with some rattlesnakes. If you lived, then God had spared you. If not, well..."

"How many people lived?" Michael asked.

"Not many. And he'd put kids in there. So when the state investigators finally showed up, the preacher and his top followers, mostly his brothers and cousins, committed suicide by snake."

"Cleopatra style," Stacey said.

"I don't think they meant it as an homage to Cleopatra, though." We reached the overgrown church wall, thick with poison ivy, and I pointed over it at the ruins of an old church. Even in the daytime, it was shrouded in shadows.

"They did the group suicide by snake right there, huh?" Stacey shivered as she looked at the ruins.

I moved my finger slightly to point at a loose cluster of boulders near the old church. "And they're buried right there. They always used boulders and rocks, saying that any fancy carved headstones were a sign of vanity."

"So all those boulders are graves?" Michael asked.

"Great spot for a picnic!" Stacey said, but no one supported her on this.

"Let's get it over with." I pulled on my gloves and climbed the old rock wall with its covering of toxic plant life.

If it was cold outside the walls, it was arctic

inside them. The tree life was thinner here than in the surrounding woods, with many of the trees standing dead among the graves, but the area seemed to get no extra sunlight because of it.

"Ugh," Jacob said, joining us, his psychic senses probably going haywire. "You definitely found your own private hell for those you condemn."

"We only put the worst ones here," I said, defensively. "The ones we can't just let roam free. Who knows what happens to them after that? They could still move on eventually, right?"

"If not, they'll grow ever more crazed inside their traps," Jacob said.

"The battery dies eventually. Then it's just the leaded glass keeping them inside. And all the graveyard dirt. And the walls of the graveyard."

"And the spirit of Reverend Blake and his pals," Stacey said. "They're tough, and they run this joint."

"I can see that." Jacob nodded. "I wouldn't want to be here during a new moon. Or a full moon. Or at night, generally. We should really getting out of here."

We found a spot by the wall and dug. Michael did most of the work, more or less insisting on it, and I was definitely more than okay with that.

We put the two traps in deep. Michael looked down at them—one cylinder containing a pair of wedding rings, including a huge diamond on Piper's ring—and the other containing a very small, bloodstained golden goblet.

"I don't think I want to know," Michael finally decided, then heaved dirt down on top of them.

Much later, the dirty work behind us in both time and distance, we stopped in a lower, warmer meadow and snacked. At some point Jacob and Stacey wandered out of sight, I assume to re-enact their favorite *Highlander* fight scene or something.

"You're okay, though, really?" Michael asked me in a low, quiet voice.

"Oh, yep. I'm just worried that Stacey's picnic blanket is going to drown the local plant life." Her checkered blanket seemed to go on for acres around us.

"How did she even fit it in her backpack?" he asked. "She had other things in there, too."

"We'll have to watch when she puts it away."

"Seriously, how have you been? Aside from the picnic blanket and the weeds beneath it?"

"You mean wildflowers?"

He kept looking at me expectantly.

I sighed. "Are you my therapist now?"

"I'm unlicensed, but I'm cheap."

"An unbeatable combination."

"I know you've been through a lot—"

"We both went through a lot. So did your sister. How is she handling things?"

"Nightmares about fires and burning buildings. More anger and resentment than usual. Ready to launch off to college in the fall and leave her miserable past behind."

"Maybe she needs therapy."

"If you know someone who won't think talking about supernatural possession is itself a sign of a mental disorder."

"Yeah, that's always a problem." I picked burrs off the ragged knee of my jeans. "I'm glad you care, really. Maybe I'm not used to that. Maybe I kind of don't expect happiness to last. Or people." I didn't say anything aloud about my parents dying when I was fifteen, but it was there, unspoken, like a dark cloud hanging over my life. Like always.

"I know something about that," Michael said. His father had left when he and his sister were young, and his mother had died only a few years ago. "We all lose people, if we live long enough. And nobody ever really expects it. It's the hardest part of my job, the ones you can't save. You see the faces of the survivors, the family members who are just beginning to understand that someone is gone. Yours was worse than normal because you didn't have many years with your parents."

"We don't have to make this about wallowing in sad memories," I said. "Let's make it a deep, profound conversation about the impermanence of all things and the preciousness of each unique moment."

"That's what I'm calling my overpriced greeting card store. Unique Moments."

"See? You can use humor to deflect from serious topics, too. I'm rubbing off on you."

"We're rubbing off on each other," he said.

I was working on something to say back to that, but his bright green eyes linked into mine, and it occurred to me that, yes, I had been quite alone in some ways for several days now, in a dark and scary place—and now we were alone together in this early-spring meadow, and we still had a little time before we had to go home. Those *Highlander* re-enactments could go on a while.

Michael leaned in close, his lips touched mine, and he was so warm against me, after so many nights of facing the icy cold world of the dead.

The feeling was electric. I both relished and distrusted it. But that was probably my natural loner instinct, more comfortable falling into trouble than into love, like some character in a David Allan Coe song. Maybe it was time to think about changing, to be more grateful for what I had, to see the beauty in life despite the pain, like some character in a Dolly Parton song.

Above, the sky was blue but going purple, the earliest reds and golds of sunset beginning to bloom. For a time, all thoughts of ghosts were chased away from my mind.

FROM THE AUTHOR

I hope you enjoyed this return to the spooky world of Ellie Jordan and friends! I've long wanted to write a story about a haunted library, so this was certainly fun for me. It was nice to get back to Ellie and Stacey after a bit of a hiatus while I worked on some other projects.

The next book concerns a haunted campground and should be out a few months after this one. I hope you'll join in for more haunted adventures! The book is called *The Trailwalker.*

Also, if you're enjoying the series, I hope you'll consider taking time to recommend the books to someone who might like them, or to rate or review it at your favorite ebook retailer.

Here are my usual links:

Newsletter (http://eepurl.com/mizJH)
Website (www.jlbryanbooks.com)
Facebook (J. L. Bryan's Books)

Thanks for reading!

Printed by Amazon Italia Logistica S.r.l.
Torrazza Piemonte (TO), Italy

13778181R00169